STAR OF LUÍS

STAR OF LUÍS

MARC TALBERT

CLARION BOOKS
New York

Clarion Books
a Houghton Mifflin Company imprint
215 Park Avenue South, New York, NY 10003
Copyright © 1999 by Marc Talbert

Type is 13-pt. Eldorado Display.
Design by Marilyn Granald.

Printed in the USA.

Library of Congress Cataloging-in-Publication Data
Talbert, Marc, 1953–
Star of Luís / by Marc Talbert
p.   cm.
Summary: Just after the bombing of Pearl Harbor, a Mexican American boy goes
with his mother from Los Angeles to New Mexico to meet her family for the first
time, and, while there, he discovers his family's hidden Jewish heritage.
ISBN 0-395-91423-X
Mexican Americans—Juvenile fiction.   [1. Mexican Americans—Fiction.
2. Jews—United States—Fiction.   3. Prejudices—Fiction.
4. New Mexico—Fiction.   5. Los Angeles (Calif.)—Fiction.]
I. Title.
PZ7.T14145St   1999
[Fic]—dc21   98–22064
                                                                                CIP
                                                                                AC

QBP   10   9   8   7   6   5   4   3   2   1

for
Buzz and Jean Bainbridge
and
Ted and Clarissa Farnsworth

Many thanks to
Stan Hordes, who brings humanity to history
Ron Hubert
Tom and Mary Belle Snow
Irwin Moore
Fernando Cubilas of Olmos Productions
Manny Zellman
Gloria Trujillo
Mario Soto
The Las Vegas, New Mexico, Public Library
Eleanor Romo
Tom Chavez
Florence Jaramillo
Saul Cohen

PART ONE

EAST LOS ANGELES

CHAPTER ONE

―――――◆―――――

"Think he saw us?" Luís gasped as he ran behind Eduardo, loosening the noose of his tie.

"*God?*" Eduardo grunted, struggling with his own tie. "He sees everything, don't He? 'Specially in church?"

Luís hadn't been thinking about God. "Think Father O'Higgins saw us, *ese?*"

If Father O'Higgins saw them, he'd be worse to deal with than God. Until he'd started going to catechism, Luís had thought of Father O'Higgins as the Father in "Father, Son, and Holy Ghost." The noose popped over his head.

"Don't think so," Eduardo puffed, still pulling at his tie.

Rounding a corner, losing sight of the church, Luís could almost hear the *chunk* of the hymnal, knocked down by his elbow from the pew in front of them when they were sneaking out.

Luckily they'd been in back of the church, off to the side, away from anybody except a zoot-suited pachuco and his slinky, red-lipped *ruca*. When the hymnal hit the floor, the boys did too, crawling up the outside aisle before bolting through the front door. He'd never seen a pachuco smile like that.

With a monumental grunt, Eduardo pulled the tie over his head.

Luís heard stumbling piano music coming from an open window as they approached Stan's house. It could only be Stan practicing the same piece of music he'd been stuck on for months. Each time Stan made a mistake, he stopped and repeated himself. Stan had the mistakes down cold.

Eduardo wagged his middle finger at the house as they ran by. "Sissy!" he yelled.

The music stopped. Luís cringed, ducked his head, and ran past Eduardo. Jeez, he missed Stan! Before he and Eduardo had started going to catechism and Stan had started going to classes at the synagogue on Breen Street, the three of them had been best friends for as long as Luís could remember.

They turned into an alley that smelled of burned garbage as they passed fifty-five-gallon drums riddled with holes, used as incinerators. Some of the sheds they passed smelled of oil and rotten wood and paint. Twice they ran through a faint stink that came from two outhouses that hadn't been torn down and were rarely used except by boys sneaking smokes, maybe with trousers around their ankles and maybe not.

As he ran, Luís wondered why he'd let Eduardo talk him into skipping Mass for the third Sunday in a row. It was only a matter of time before Eduardo's parents found out. Luís hated knowing that Eduardo's mother would think he was less than perfect. Besides, left to himself, he would have stayed.

Luís liked Mass. He always had. The squeaking pews made bat noises and the Latin words echoed softly among the arches that touched like praying fingertips over the altar. He liked the foggy organ music and he liked watching people, especially girls—although Eduardo said girls who went to Mass weren't the kind you could have fun with. And there was that gauzy light draping itself over the body of Christ hanging above the altar, shifting with the sun, making Christ's loincloth seem to sway. Luís even liked watching the few men at Mass (looking guilty or bored) and staring at the clumps of old women in black, who raced through prayers and hymns with loud, cackling voices.

Stan would have understood, even if he was a Jew. Eduardo, on the other hand, would have just laughed and called Luís a goody-goody—laughed and told him that someday, if he wasn't careful, he'd become a priest, and then his nuts would fall off.

They crossed the last street before Eduardo's backyard.

"Beat you!" Eduardo shouted, pulling ahead of Luís. Luís put on a burst of speed, but Eduardo grabbed the back door first. For someone who puffed so much, Eduardo could sure run fast when he wanted to.

Luís loved the smell of Eduardo's house, so different

5

from the smell of his own. The smell—of mole and chili and *masa*—spread to the rest of the house from the kitchen, where the boys pawed through the Frigidaire.

"Not that, *ese*," Eduardo said as Luís picked up a plate, its mound covered with waxed paper that was soft from being used many times. "It's been there for a week. *Mamacita* hates to throw anything away."

Luís nodded. "Know what ya mean." Only when she smelled something with the refrigerator door closed did Luís's mother toss it.

"Hey! Look!" Eduardo pulled a length of sausage from behind an opened quart jar of canned apricots gone milky with age. He tore it in two and handed a piece to Luís.

Luís hesitated. Seeing Eduardo's eyes squinch, he grabbed.

"You're welcome!" Eduardo growled, ripping a hunk off his own piece.

Luís lifted the sausage to his mouth, but once more he hesitated. What if it was pork? His mother often told him that his whole family, from way back, got sick if they ate pork.

"What's wrong? Gone snooty on me?" Eduardo sometimes thought Luís's family looked down on his family because his parents came from Mexico. "Too good for *pocho* food?"

Luís shrugged. "Naw." He glanced at the sausage. A little pork shouldn't kill him if he didn't swallow. He bit off a chunk and pretended to chew, cradling the meat on his tongue. Eduardo's face relaxed. "Come on," he said, almost chummy now. "We're burnin' daylight."

Luís nodded and smiled. Saliva filled his mouth, along with a taste like scabs.

As Eduardo bolted from the kitchen, Luís spit the sausage into his hand and flipped the whole shooting match behind the refrigerator for the kitchen mice and *cucarachas*.

Eduardo was frantically unbuttoning his shirt when Luís walked into the bedroom.

"Your clothes on fire?" Luís reached underneath Eduardo's bed and pulled out the jeans and T-shirt he'd stashed there. Calmly, deliberately, he began to unbutton his own shirt.

"You're not ready in time, I'll leave without you." Eduardo turned his back to Luís before he pulled down his khakis. Luís glanced at the crucifix above Eduardo's bed. He'd never lived with one and felt uncomfortable undressing in front of Christ on His cross.

By the time Eduardo had his jeans on, Luís was just shucking his shirt. "Hope y'like walking," Eduardo huffed, rushing out.

Luís wasn't worried. The tires on Eduardo's bike were always soft. As he pulled off his khakis, he glanced at the crucifix and made the sign of the cross before turning his back to it.

As Luís expected, Eduardo was in the garage, jerking

7

up and down on the pump, looking as if he were trying to set off dynamite. His red face looked as if it might explode any moment.

Eduardo groaned and straightened his back. "Ma-a-an! *Pinche* bike!"

Luís nodded. If he'd hurried any faster, he'd have had to help with the tires. "Ready?"

Eduardo nodded and disconnected the nozzle from the tire nipple. He wheeled the bike to the alley. "I pumped. You pedal."

When they rode together, one of them straddled the bar while steering and pedaling, and the other perched on the seat. Luís hated straddling the bar. His knees sometimes buckled when they went over potholes, paralyzing him with the pain of cracked nuts.

Eduardo climbed behind him and bounced on the seat. "Burn rubber!" he shouted. Luís stomped on the pedal. The bike lurched forward, shedding rust flakes as they hit the pavement.

Why am I doing this? Luís wondered. As much as he tried to like baseball, it always seemed like a lot of waiting around just to make a fool of himself. He and Eduardo probably wouldn't be invited to play anyway. Neither of them had a glove, and the guys who played in the vacant lot across the street from the Evergreen Cemetery were mostly Jews and Negroes, with only a few Mexicans and Italians and Orientals thrown in. And they were all older.

Eduardo vaulted off just before Luís brought the bike

to a stop. "Hey!" Luís shouted, scrambling away as the bike tipped over. He left it where it fell.

The vacant lot wasn't very big, but it was big enough. Eduardo and Luís leaned against a car parked near first base and scoped out the scene.

Fabio, who had a catcher's mitt but loved to pitch, was on the mound—dirt scratched over a bald tire. "Hey!" he called toward them. "One a you beaners want t' hit while I warm up?"

"Sure!" Eduardo tried to keep the eager squeak from his voice. He trotted toward home plate. Fabio was always the leader of one team (on account of the mitt), and Eduardo wanted to impress him.

Luís scowled and leaned harder into the car, making its suspension groan. He hated people calling him a beaner.

Charlie, a Negro from the neighborhood west of the cemetery, walked toward Fabio. "What chew doin', man? He don't know nothin' about baseball." Charlie, easily the biggest kid around, was the leader of whatever team played Fabio's. Out of principle, he argued with Fabio about every little thing.

"Want me to warm up on *you?*" Fabio asked.

In answer, Charlie turned to Eduardo. "What chew waitin' for? Pick up that bat!" he barked. Eduardo picked up the bat.

Charlie yelled to Fabio. "Ben's not here. Who's gonna call 'em?" Ben never played baseball but loved to ump. And he was fair.

Fabio shrugged. "Since we don't got an ump, you get all the balls ya want, long as you're willing to chase 'em."

"Got twice as many balls as you." Charlie laughed. "An' they don't know nothin' but home runs."

Charlie and Fabio shook on it, and Charlie sauntered to his team—several Jews, a Korean, and a Mexican who was built like a brick.

Eduardo didn't hit a single ball while Fabio warmed up—but he got hit twice by wild pitches and swung at everything else.

"I'm *never* gonna bat with that maniac pitching," Luís told Eduardo back at the car. "He almost hit your head, *ese!*"

Eduardo rubbed the round of his shoulder and moved his arm like a broken wing. "At least they know how much we wanna play. Next thing y'know, someone's gonna pick us for their team."

Luís shook his head. "All they know is we don't got no sense."

"Get the game goin'," shouted Charlie.

"Who's the first victim?" called Fabio.

Luís and Eduardo watched the Korean kid walk to home plate.

"Chink, chink, chink!" a boy named Moses called from the outfield.

"Don't listen to that kike, Junho," called Charlie. "Jes' hit the ball down 'is mouth!"

10

"Who you callin' a kike, nigger?"

Disgusted, Luís shook his head at all the name calling. All it did was make the boys fight.

"Come *on*," Fabio pleaded, looking from Charlie to Moses. "Cut the crap. Let's play a little ball!"

Before anybody could play (or fight), Luís heard the sound of skidding rubber on the street. He jumped off the car he'd been leaning against.

A lone Buick stopped, slightly sideways, inches from where he'd been standing, its nose poking into the oncoming lane. Another car approached, slowing down, and Luís heard a long, angry honk. A car behind that one, taken unawares, squealed to a stop and bobbed. An angry man in a gray suit and black fedora sprang from the third car.

"What the hell's goin' on!" he shouted to the man in the Buick, who was leaning forward, unaware of the commotion he was causing. The angry man stomped up to the Buick and pounded on its hood. "Go home and sleep it off, buster!"

The man in the Buick looked up and shook his head. Slowly, seeming drunk, he got out of the car. "We've been bombed," he said.

"Hell's bells! *Who's* bombed? People like you—"

The man from the Buick raised his hand. "No. Really. Listen." He reached into his car and cranked up the radio. It sounded as if the car itself were talking, its voice rumbling and revving, words occasionally backfiring.

Several more cars had stopped by now and a small crowd gathered around the Buick, along with the boys from both baseball teams.

Luís listened. The Japanese had just bombed a bunch of American ships in a place called Pearl Harbor. In Hawaii. At dawn. There were sinking ships and burning bodies everywhere.

Wasn't Hawaii where people wore grass skirts? Luís pictured men and women and children running around hollering, their grass skirts on fire.

"Think Jap planes are headed this way?" a man asked. A woman in her Sunday best put a gloved hand to her mouth, but not before a little cry escaped.

Eduardo was already on the bike and beginning to pedal when Luís ran up and grabbed the seat, almost sending Eduardo over the handlebars.

"Come *on*! Those *pinche* Japs could be here any minute!" Eduardo puffed as Luís climbed aboard.

CHAPTER TWO

"I don't wanna *ever* hear that name again!" Luís was walking toward the cemetery with Eduardo after school the next day. It had been Pearl Harbor this and Pearl Harbor that ever since the class listened on the radio to President Roosevelt declare war on Japan in that polite, clever way of his, using big words that sounded like curses but weren't.

"Me either," Eduardo said.

When they got to the cemetery, Fabio and Charlie had already chosen up teams. All Luís and Eduardo could hope was that somebody would go home and give them a place.

"*Pinche* Japs!" Eduardo muttered, as if they were to blame for everything now. The boys leaned against the same car that they'd leaned against yesterday.

"Who's up?" Fabio shouted to Charlie, pounding the ball into his mitt.

Charlie handed the bat to the bricklike Mexican kid.

Fabio threw the first pitch. The Mexican kid didn't even flinch as it almost creamed his knees.

"Ah, ma-a-an!" Eduardo called. It was a safe thing to

yell, and he didn't want either team to forget he was available.

The car rocked, and Luís figured it was just Eduardo, bouncing on his butt. Luís turned to tell Eduardo to knock it off and saw a pachuco leaning on the front fender.

Smoke from the pachuco's cigarette gathered under the brim of his hat, which was cocked low over his forehead. Luís couldn't see the eyes that must have been looking at him. The broad shoulders of the pachuco's shimmering green zoot suit were padded and its cloth fell like a curtain to his knees. Luís found himself looking down the razor creases of the matching green pants, the cuffs tight above the tops of oversized shoes that were polished so brightly their blackness lay deep beneath the surface of whatever they reflected.

And then he knew. His eyes flicked up. It was the same pachuco who'd smiled at him in church. Why was he in this neighborhood? It could only mean trouble. There were people in this part of town who would have loved to thump on a pachuco.

The man nodded, barely, and Luís swallowed, trying to smile.

"You crawl real good," the pachuco said, surprisingly soft and low.

On his other side, Luís heard Eduardo gasp. "What you doin' here, Ricardo?" Luís stared. Eduardo knew this man?

The pachuco tipped his head back to better see Eduardo. "Checkin' out the old neighborhood, *ese,*" he

14

said. "Your brother says *hola.*" And then, nodding toward the game, he asked, "That *gabacho* always pitch 'em wild for *la raza?*" Not waiting for an answer, he continued. "You wanna hit home runs, you gotta make 'em pitch it the way *you* want it. *¿Comprende?* The way *you* want it."

The pachuco took a drag of his cigarette and spit the butt from his mouth. It flew to the ground and smoldered. He peered at Luís and Eduardo, his mouth tight. For a moment the smoke cleared under the brim of his hat, and Luís saw how nervous his eyes were. "See you in church," he said, and walked away, the silver chain that looped from inside his jacket swinging around his shin.

Just when the game was sputtering to life, Junho appeared. He walked to home plate as Charlie was getting ready to bat.

"Need another player?" Junho asked, as if he didn't see Eduardo and Luís were already waiting.

"We doin' fine," said Charlie.

"Yeah," Fabio called from the mound. "We don't play with no Japs."

As if he hadn't heard, Junho stepped closer. "Can I play?"

Charlie turned to Junho. "Tha's a mighty dangerous place fo' a Jap." He stuck the bat out, wagging it at Junho.

"I'm *not* Japanese," Junho yelled. "My family's from Korea."

By this time Fabio had walked halfway from the pitcher's mound. "He look yellow to you?" he asked

15

Charlie. "Looks yellow to me. Yellow means Jap in my book. So scram, Jap."

"I ain't no Jap, so lay off. I just wanna play!"

"You don' hear too good, do ya?" Charlie took a menacing step toward Junho, poking the bat into Junho's stomach.

"Neither do you," said Junho. "I . . . HATE . . . Japs!" And then, to everybody's surprise, he leapt onto Charlie, fists swinging.

When Junho went down for the last time, Charlie spit on him. "An' that's fo' Pearl Harbor," he said.

It made Luís queasy to see Junho lying on his back, blood trickling from his nose, spittle on his face, shaking his head and crying. Who could tell the difference—Japanese or Korean? Could somebody look like a Jap and be something else?

Frayed ribbons of clouds looked as if they were snagged on palm trees and power poles as Luís and Eduardo walked home, silent, stepping around slugs that were sliding from the grass onto the cooling sidewalk. It often happened that the boys would be lost in their own thoughts and then, within sight of one of their houses, fifteen minutes of thinking would get stuffed, like too big a bite, into a couple minutes of frantic jawing.

"How old d'you hafta be to join the army?" Eduardo asked.

16

"Don't know. Eighteen, I s'pose."

"Sure hope the war lasts long enough so's I can fight. Be my *pinche* luck if it didn't."

They were nearing Eduardo's house.

"Think that pachuco had a knife?" Luís asked.

"Sure. Don't they all?" Eduardo answered. Luís nodded. Eduardo should know. His older brother, Fernando, had been kicked out of the house for using all his money to buy a zoot suit like Ricardo's so he could hang out with his buddies.

As they came up the alley in back of his house, Eduardo moaned, stopping. "I forgot!"

"Forgot what?"

"*La vieja* wanted me home right after school—to get ready for Mass—for the friggin' Feast of the Immaculate Conception."

"That's tonight?" Father O'Higgins had talked about it at catechism last week, and Luís still got the creeps thinking that God could knock up the Virgin Mary just by looking at her. If he were a girl, he'd be scared stiff of God looking at him.

Eduardo nodded. "This morning *Mamacita* said it was a good sign if the war started today. She said that we're gonna win, what with the Virgin being with child and all."

"Maybe if you run, you'll make it to church before the war's over," Luís said. He wished his mother sometimes went to church and wanted him to go with her.

"Ah, blow it out your . . ."

"See you mañana," Luís interrupted.

Luís wanted to fall asleep. How could he, with his mother rocking in her chair, pinching squeaks from the floor? His father still wasn't home, and he knew she was worried that Immigration was at it again, shipping people who looked Mexican across the border, not believing those who said they were American.

What was his father doing? Had Immigration nabbed him?

Luís tried lying on his back, his stomach, and both sides. He jammed the pillow between his legs, under his head, and over his head. Nothing helped. He couldn't stop thinking of the last time his father hadn't come home before bedtime.

It must have been five months ago. His father had gone to a union meeting, thinking it wouldn't hurt to listen. His father had left in disgust. But his boss at the brick factory had been lurking outside in a car. The next day, his father had been fired.

Luís sighed and closed his eyes. Mercifully, before long a velvet darkness closed like a curtain over the front of his brain.

It was night and Luís found himself standing at the front of an open boat, not knowing where water turned to sky. The boat creaked as it rode the waves.

From his left came the drone of many airplanes, sounding like a radio's vacuum tubes warming up. He saw shadows, darker than the sky. The *pinche* Japs on their way to bomb Pearl Harbor?

A wave lifted the front of the boat and his gaze lifted with it. Planes were overhead, and he punched the air with his fist.

"Go home!" he cried.

As if they heard him, the buzzing shadows looped back. The first bomb struck to his right. The explosion nearly knocked him off his feet. The sound was followed by chunks of water, blazing with light, hissing as they splattered on him.

"Cowards!" he cried. The planes circled again. More bombs fell, but waves, grown huge with explosions, protected him.

"You'll live in infamy!" he screamed, liking the sound of President Roosevelt's words. If he, Luís, kept them angry, maybe the Japs would drop all their bombs now, leaving none for Pearl Harbor. Maybe he could save America from war!

A bomb came toward him, wobbling. A direct hit? Luís flinched as it smacked water behind him.

The boat rose, riding the crest of a swelling sound. As the water fell away, the boat shot through the air, aimed at an airplane that was aimed at him.

He closed his eyes, bracing for the crash. . . .

* * *

Luís's head hit the floor with a thud. His skin was slippery with sweat and his stomach gurgled.

He was not at sea. He heard his father snoring from his parents' bedroom.

From the other end of the house came the squeaks of his mother's rocking chair, sounding like the boat in his dream as it bucked waves. His legs unsteady, he got to his feet and tumbled back into bed.

CHAPTER THREE

———————◆———————

Still in bed, Luís heard his father's voice come from his parents' bedroom. Luís couldn't make out the words or his mother's sharp reply.

His mother didn't smile as she walked past his door. "Time to get up!" Her lips pinched off each word as it came out.

While Luís pulled on his jeans his father walked by, bumping the far side of the hallway with his shoulder.

"You feeling OK?" Luís asked, entering the kitchen, sitting opposite his father.

His father groaned. "I feel like a mule kicked me last night." His voice was as rough as his face, and the words came out as if he had stubble on his tongue.

"Mules don't kick themselves," Luís's mother snapped, banging yesterday's coffee grounds onto newspaper.

"They do if they drink tequila," his father replied.

His mother turned, pot in hand, looking at Luís's father but speaking to Luís. "Your father has something to tell you."

"Not now." Luís's father shook his head.

"Yes. Now. Or have you decided you made a mistake?"

Luís's mother turned to the counter, folding the newspaper over the grounds, making a brown-stained pillow.

His father closed his eyes. "I have a new job."

"Yeah?" Luís leaned forward.

"In the army."

"You joined up?"

"Yep. To fight for truth, justice, and the American way."

"Did you get drunk before or after you signed up?"

Luís looked at his mother, who was measuring coffee into the metal nest that stood on one leg inside the pot.

"They wouldn't've taken me if I'd been drunk. Look. Ever'where I went, people were talkin' about joinin' up— even people with good jobs!"

His mother set the pot on a crown of flame. "Why didn't you let *them* join and then take one of *their* good jobs?"

Hissing water steamed off the pot. Coffee began to percolate into the little glass bubble in the center of the lid.

Luís's father shook his head. "Y'know what? They almost didn't take me. One man asked for my blue papers, like maybe I was from Mexico."

The coffee was more frantic now, the glass bubble darker brown with each *bu-bump-bum-bum-bu-bump*.

"For once, I wish you *were* from Mexico!" his mother

cried. Tears streamed down her face. "Who's going to take care of *us* while you fight?"

Luís looked in alarm at his mother and father (whose face was as red as his eyes now), and at the coffeepot that sounded almost ready to boil over.

"Don't be surprised if I go back to New Mexico!" his mother yelled, grabbing the pot as foaming coffee began to seep from under the lid.

"Where the chickens are smarter than the people?"

"Where we have family!"

His mother put her face in her free hand and sobbed. The pot tipped. Coffee leapt from the spout and splattered at her feet.

"You think the *pinche* Japs are gonna bomb Los Angeles?" It was Wednesday, and Luís and Eduardo were walking home from school, where their teacher, Miss Standish, had spent a good part of the day talking about air-raid drills.

"Naw." Luís knew this wasn't the answer Eduardo wanted to hear and not the answer he himself believed.

"What about those Jap planes people say they saw?" Some older kids claimed it had been in the newspaper— Japanese planes north of Los Angeles.

"Could've been flies—bi-i-g flies."

Eduardo wasn't in the mood for jokes. "What about the radio stations?" Yesterday, all radio stations had been silent for almost twenty hours, and nobody knew why. Without news (or music or even static), people had made up stories of enemy boats offshore and Japanese soldiers crawling through the hills behind Santa Monica toward Hollywood.

"How should *I* know?"

"What's the signal for an air raid?" Eduardo asked, trying to sound as if he were testing Luís.

"Three minutes."

Eduardo nodded, pretending he'd known. "The all clear?"

"One minute."

"The blackout signal?" Eduardo was no longer pretending.

"Three blasts."

"Jeez! By the time I learn all that stuff the war'll be over. Miss Standish will never pick me to be one of those whatchamacallits—the ones who wear badges and carry gas masks and boss people around when we're being attacked!"

They walked in silence to the front yard of Eduardo's house. "Wanna come inside? Mess around?" Eduardo's mother had told him to come right home, in case the Japanese attacked.

"Can't. My old man wants to take me Christmas shopping."

"Ah, come *on*! For just a little while?"

"See you mañana!" Luís trotted down the sidewalk.

"If the Japs don't get you first!" Eduardo made the sound of a machine gun.

It was a lie about shopping with his dad. But Eduardo would never have given up if Luís had told him the truth—that he was going Christmas shopping *for* his mom and dad. As he walked toward Brooklyn Avenue, he felt inside the pocket of his jeans. All his money was there: a buck thirty-three.

Last night he'd asked his mother what she thought his father might want. "Something we can look at, something that will make us think of him," she'd said. And then he'd asked his father what he thought his mother would like. "A plant—something with flowers," he'd said.

Their answers made Luís think of the Christmas cactus Eduardo's mother kept in the windowsill above her kitchen sink.

The bell rang when he opened the door of the gift shop. The saleslady behind the counter looked up and was about to go back to reading when Luís walked toward a row of plants by the front window.

"How much?" he asked, pointing.

The saleslady slipped around the counter and walked past him. "This one?"

"No. Next to it."

She picked it up and felt its soil. "A dollar and ten cents." Seeing the surprise on his face, she added, "The pot's from England. And this one will bloom for

Christmas." She held it toward him. Its flower buds were like little pink carrots at the tip of each glossy, scalloped limb.

"Does it cost extra for a bow?"

She raised her eyebrows. "A present?"

He nodded.

"Nothing extra for the bow," she said, taking it to the counter. As she made a spool of ribbon blossom in her hands, she told him how to take care of it. "Too much sunlight will send it into shock," she said. "If it begins to wilt, water it—but not too much. Too much water is as bad as too little."

Luís never knew taking care of a plant was so complicated.

He tried to keep the plant in shade as he walked home. After a few blocks he began to worry that it was wilting. He felt the soil. Was it too dry? Would it look like seaweed by the time he got home?

Ahead, no more than a half block away, he saw the church. He hoped it wasn't a sin to think what he was thinking.

Inside, the church was cool and shadowy. He walked to the font of holy water and dipped his finger. He made the sign of the cross and then dipped again, sprinkling water around the plant. He did this several times.

Feeling thirsty himself, he dipped once more, and stuck out his tongue.

It quivered like a touched slug. Instead of tasting like a drop of heaven, the holy water tasted sour as sweat. He forced himself to swallow, almost gagging.

Just then the organ started playing, its sound coming from every direction.

Swallowing again, trying to rid his mouth of the water's taste, he stepped into the sound, off to the side. Candles in red glasses, sitting in stepped racks to the right of the altar, seemed to flicker with the music's rhythm. Luís looked above the altar, toward the arches. He wouldn't have been surprised to see the music swirling like the oily smoke of incense, but all he saw were dust motes, looking like the ghosts of dead flies darting into and out of candied light from the stained-glass windows.

It wasn't the first time he'd wondered what it would be like to live and work in a church. What would it be like to be a priest? To know the answers to everything?

He stared at the crucifix. Was being a priest worth having your nuts fall off?

His eye caught movement. He turned to see his father walk past him and down the main aisle. Luís watched him genuflect and then slide into a pew. His head was bowed and his shoulders hunched.

Luís had never known his father to visit church by himself.

Why? As if in answer, Luís thought of boot camp.

Until now, it had never occurred to him that his

father might be scared of leaving for boot camp tomorrow.

Luís wished he hadn't seen. He didn't want his father to know that he knew. Clutching the plant, he hurried outside.

CHAPTER FOUR

Luís sat on the edge of his bed, staring at the Christmas cactus, thinking. Maybe it wasn't such a good idea for his father to join the army. He wished that he was waiting for his father to come home from the brick factory, his clothes so caked with clay that he'd had to be hosed off at the back door.

That had been Luís's job. And after Luís had hosed him off once, his father would strip to his BVDs to be hosed down again. Luís always enjoyed spraying his father, jamming his thumb into the hose, trying to tickle him with ribbons of water. It had been fun to watch the clay melt, sliding off his father's chest and stomach, the pouch of his BVDs swelling to the point of bursting with water that collected behind the layer of clay trapped inside.

He heard the kitchen screen door slapping shut and then his father's muffled voice.

"Time for dinner!" his mother called.

Luís picked up the plant and walked to the kitchen.

He forced himself to smile as he handed the plant to his father. "Since you might not be here—Merry

Christmas. For Mom too. And," he added, "the pot's from England."

Luís was pleased to see that he'd surprised both his parents. His father cleared his throat. "Thanks, Luís."

"How beautiful!" His mother's hands trembled as she took the plant and pecked him on the forehead. He tried to remember the last time his mother had worn perfume. He couldn't.

Luís and his father sat in their usual places while his mother brought food to the table.

"Don't imagine I'll get food like this in the army," his father said. He got up to help his wife sit in her chair with an awkwardness that came from little practice.

"This calls for a celebration!" His father went to the cabinet where he kept a jug of wine he called Dago red. Bringing two jelly glasses to the table, he wiggled out the cork and poured.

"I don't think so—" his mother protested.

"To us," his father interrupted. He lifted a glass, took a sip, and sighed. Luís's mother took a sip and sneezed.

As they ate, Luís was alarmed to see his mother down her wine in three gulps. When his father finished his, he poured more for both of them.

"Another toast," his father said. "To the new man of the house." He looked at Luís. "I'm countin' on you."

It was then the siren down the block went off.

Were the Japs attacking?

When the siren stopped, they sat, stunned.

"What the hell . . ." his father finally said.

It came again.

"BLACKOUT!" Luís shouted.

His father stared, nodded, and then flicked the kitchen's light switch. Darkness and quiet came at the same moment.

"Should I—" his mother began.

The third and final blast overwhelmed her question.

"How'd you know what kind of signal it was?" his father whispered when everything was mercifully quiet.

"School."

"We should turn on the radio," his mother said. "They might have some news."

And then came the all-clear blast.

"It's safe now," Luís shouted.

Luís's father flicked on the light. The siren was replaced by the rumble of cars, seeming louder than usual, as if making up for lost time.

Luís lay in bed, listening. He'd never heard his mother snore before. But then he'd never before seen her drink wine like she had at dinner.

Stockinged footsteps approached, and his father's shape filled the doorway.

"You're awake?"

"Yeah."

His father stepped into the room. "Sit down?"

"Sure."

The bed groaned. "Thanks for the plant, Luís."

"Sure."

"I'm proud of you—knowing what to do tonight."

"Thanks."

"I'll write."

Luís felt as if he were watching a movie, only he'd never felt like crying during a movie, no matter how sappy things got.

"I'll take care of her," Luís said, trying to sound brave, light from the hallway glinting on the tears that were puddling in his eyes.

"I know you will." His father hesitated and then leaned forward, kissing the top of Luís's head.

Something brushed against Luís's face. As his father straightened up, Luís saw the glint of a cross as it swung back into the top of his father's pajamas, disappearing.

"Good night, Luís." His father stood.

"Good night," Luís croaked, blinking.

Only after the hallway light went out did Luís let the tears flow. Never in all those years of hosing off his father had Luís seen his father wear a cross. Never.

Before catechism, he'd thought wearing a cross, or making the sign of the cross, meant "Cross my heart and hope to die." Christ had gone out of His way to die. He'd *wanted* to die, so He could save everyone.

His father wouldn't have to die to save America, would he?

A taste like holy water filled his mouth.

Closing his eyes, he pictured his father being hosed off at the end of the day. The clay ran off, thick and oily, and his skin shone red. Slowly at first, and then faster, his father's skin began to slough off, dripping in thick mudlike globs, showing muscle and bones and guts. Blood ran into his BVDs, turning them bright red.

Before the pouch exploded, Luís opened his eyes.

CHAPTER FIVE

"Wanna see what I'm gettin' for Christmas?" Eduardo asked for the gazillionth time in two days. With two weeks until Christmas, Eduardo had finally figured out where his mother was hiding the presents.

"Come *on*!" Luís said. "How many times I gotta tell ya? My momma wants me to check our mail and then check with her at the Blochs' house."

"Aw, come on yourself, *ese*! Just a peek!"

What would it take to make Eduardo give up? Luís kicked at the sidewalk in frustration.

"Your momma still 'fraid of the Japs?"

Luís scowled, not saying anything. The day his father left, there had been another Japanese bombing raid somewhere around Hawaii. The Sunday after, the governor declared a state of emergency, saying not to worry—he just needed extra power in case of trouble, which he said there wouldn't be. It sounded as if the governor didn't know what he was talking about.

But the cherry on top was when the kids in school were registered the following morning. "A precaution,"

Miss Standish had told them, "in case of"—and she made what followed sound like the title of a radio soap opera—"Air Raids or Evacuation."

"Maybe she still thinks your dad's gonna write every day?"

"Leave my father outta it!"

They glared at each other, their lips welded, their hands fisted.

Truth to tell, Luís would have loved doing almost anything rather than checking the mail and going to the Blochs'. Mail or no mail, once he got there his mother put him to work—walking the Blochs' dog, Princess, or tending the Blochs' baby, Adam.

Luís's hands relaxed first. "Tell ya what. I'll come in, see whatcha got, if you come with me after."

Eduardo's eyes narrowed.

"Well?" Luís knew it would be hard for Eduardo to decide between showing him the glove and checking out the ball game across from the cemetery.

Eduardo sighed and his mouth relaxed enough to form a tight smile. "Deal."

Eduardo's mother was halfway up to her elbows in *masa* for tamales as they walked through the kitchen. She looked up so quickly, several drops of sweat fell from her face, seasoning the dough. "*¡Hola, hijos!*"

"Hi!" Eduardo called over his shoulder. Luís glanced at the Christmas cactus in her window. Compared with the one at his house, it looked pathetic. Maybe the holy water had helped the one he'd given his mom and dad stay healthy.

They hurried down the hall to Eduardo's parents' bedroom. Everything in it smelled of some kind of sweet powder, and the curtains matched the bedspread. Luís had a hard time imagining Eduardo's father sleeping there.

Eduardo didn't need to look as he reached under the bedspread and pulled out a box wrapped in red-and-green tartan-patterned paper. The tape hardly stuck anymore. When Eduardo slipped off the green ribbon, the paper fell open by itself.

"A beauty, isn't it." With reverence, Eduardo held out a baseball glove.

"Yeah," Luís said, slipping its oily richness over his left hand. He tried flexing his fingers, feeling jealous. Even though he didn't like baseball that much, this glove must have cost a bundle. And it felt and smelled great. He took it off and watched Eduardo rewrap it. "What else ya gettin'?"

"A shirt *la vieja* made of the same cloth she used to make a shirt for my father. And a book."

"And your mother?"

"A pair of shoes—" Eduardo stopped, looking as if he'd been tricked. "Come *on*," he said, a rare show of guilt on his face. "Let's grab a cookie and go before *la vieja* figures out what we been doing."

* * *

As they approached the mailbox at Luís's house, Eduardo pointed to the blue star that was taped to the inside of their front window. Blue stars were popping up on windows all over the neighborhood, wherever somebody was in the armed forces.

"Who made that for ya, anyway?"

"My mom." Luís had watched her make it with two triangles on top of each other. It was an easy kind of star to make, unlike the kind that had only five points that never looked even.

"Got too many points."

Luís reached into the mailbox. "My dad's worth an extra point."

Incredibly, his hand touched a letter.

"From your old man?"

It was addressed to his mother, in handwriting Luís didn't recognize. "No." He slipped it into his back pocket.

"We're goin' to a Jew house, right?"

"Know any Mexicans with maids?" Luís snapped in reply. Even if it was a Jew house, Luís wished his house was more like the Blochs'—comfortable and quiet. There the light seemed especially quiet—slipping through lace curtains or seeping from lampshades or sparkling as if it were seltzer spilling over frosted glass fixtures that hung like punch bowls from the ceiling.

"Ya know why they're called Jews, don'cha?" Before Luís could say anything, Eduardo continued. "'Cause they bury jewels and gold all over the place. *Jew*-els," Eduardo said, exaggerating his mouth as he spoke. "Get it? Ever look for where the Blochs bury their gold and jewels?"

"No." Luís pictured the spot where Eduardo hid his money. "Maybe they bury it in their garage, in a coffee can."

Eduardo laughed. "I ain't no Jew."

Luís grinned. "Naw. You eat too many beans and tortillas."

"About time!" Holding a paring knife, Luís's mother looked from Luís to Eduardo, and then back to Luís.

"Sorry." Reaching for the letter, hoping it would distract her, he held it out. "For you."

She took it and nodded toward Adam, who was in his playpen, gumming a carrot. "His diaper needs changing."

"Aw, Mom!" How could she embarrass him like that in front of his best friend? What would Eduardo think, him doing girl stuff?

"Don't 'Mom' me!" She slit the letter open with her knife.

Eduardo poked him in the arm. "What we waitin' for?" he asked, with a fakey kind of jolliness.

Luís shrugged. He walked to the playpen and picked Adam up. Princess got up from her wicker bed in the corner and led them from the kitchen, as if she were in charge.

Luís lay Adam on the large braided oval rug in the middle of the bedroom. "Get a diaper for me?"

"Thought Adam was the one needing a diaper."

"Fun-n-ny, *carnal.*"

"Thanks. Where?"

"Over there." As he turned and pointed, Princess jammed her nose into Adam's diaper and sniffed. "Cut it out!" Luís pushed the dog off. She was always doing that!

Eduardo handed the diaper to Luís. "Why don't you let her lick him clean? Bet it's like doggy chocolate."

Luís shook his head. "Sick, Eduardo." He undid a pin and slipped it out. As he undid the other one, Eduardo leaned almost as close to Adam's diaper as Princess had.

"What *you* doin'?" Luís asked. "Gonna fight Princess for doggy chocolate?"

"Just wanna see if his pecker's different."

"Oh." Luís remembered the first time he saw Adam's penis—unlike his own, Adam's was a small pinkish mushroom, poking out from a collar of tattered skin. It looked as if Princess had tried to lick Adam clean and gotten carried away—done that brisk chewing thing with her little front teeth she did when grooming herself. Had she bit some of it off? It must have hurt like hell.

He lifted the diaper's front.

"Jeez." Eduardo held his nose. "My poppa was right about Jews doing a . . . a circumference on their boys' peckers." He turned to Luís. "Mind gettin' rid of the stink?"

Luís grabbed Adam by both ankles, lifting his butt and wiping it off with the wet front part of the diaper. He

39

pulled out the dirty diaper and slipped the clean one in its place.

As Luís reached for the pins, Eduardo said, "Check out his head. Right here." He reached up and rubbed the top of Luís's head, on either side. "Feel for horns—here and—here."

"Cut the crap, *ese*," Luís said. "Jews don't have no horns."

"Wanna bet? My poppa says Jews are born with bumps—like baby goats have."

"Get serious!"

Eduardo nodded. "*De veras.* Sometimes they hafta be cut off. Why d'you think so many Jews wear those skull cap things?"

Luís had wondered about those caps too. And what would it hurt to feel the top of Adam's head? Adam giggled as Luís touched him.

"How're you doing?"

Luís looked up and saw his mother standing in the doorway, frowning. He slid his hand away, hoping she didn't know what he'd been doing.

"Fine."

"Take Princess for a walk. I'll finish up here," she said.

Luís looked at his mother as he stood. Had she been crying?

* * *

40

Luís held the leash tight. Who was taking who for a walk, anyway?

"You didn't feel *anything*?" Eduardo asked again.

"No."

"You sure? Not even a little, bitty something?"

"I've felt more lumps on an egg." They turned up Breen Street. Ahead was the big brick synagogue. Its big stained-glass window was lit up, showing a star with six points, the same as his mother's.

"Maybe they'll pop out when he gets older," Eduardo groused.

It struck Luís just after they turned the corner. The synagogue's star had shone golden. Miss Standish had told them that gold stars in windows meant—how did she say it?—"Death in the Service of Our Country."

What had been in the letter? Was his father all right?

Luís began running, passing Princess, dragging her a couple of steps before she leapt past him, enjoying this new game.

"Hey!" Eduardo shouted. "Wait up!"

Luís ran all the way to the Blochs's house.

"Your mother has already left," Mrs. Blochs said. She didn't sound pleased.

Luís gulped air. The letter. His father. Could he be wounded already?

"Here." Mrs. Blochs pulled a small purse from the larger purse on the kitchen table. She poked around and pulled out a coin. "Thank you for walking Princess." She held it out.

Luís hesitated. What was going on? She'd never paid him for his help before. Was she feeling sorry for him?

Eduardo reached from behind and took the nickel from a surprised Mrs. Blochs. "Thanks, Señora. Any time."

Outside, Eduardo ran beside Luís, puffing. "What's . . . gotten . . . into . . . you?"

Luís was breathing too hard to answer. All he could think about was the letter and the gold star. As they passed Eduardo's house, the puffing stopped.

"Watch out for Japs!" he heard Eduardo call. "And thanks for the nickel!"

His mother was in the kitchen, sitting at the table, staring at the letter. She looked up, startled, as he rushed in.

"What's it say?" Luís managed to gasp.

"My father's sick. He may not live much longer."

Luís felt his legs go rubbery in relief.

His mother's mouth quivered, and her eyes filled with tears.

"I'm sorry." He tried to sound sad but how could he care about somebody he'd never met?

Tears spilled as his mother continued. "I told Mrs. Blochs I quit. She told me they're going to move to Silver Lake soon, anyway, across the river."

Luís walked to his mother. He put a trembling hand

42

on her shoulder. He wanted to say something strong and sure, something like what his father would have said. But he didn't trust his voice.

CHAPTER SIX

Eduardo was trying to raise the seat of his bike so his feet wouldn't drag. But his crescent wrench was stripped and the nut was rusted.

Luís watched for a few minutes. "Want some help?"

Eduardo ignored Luís, banging to loosen the nut.

Luís was tempted to go home. What would it take to make Eduardo less crabby? It wasn't *his* fault that Luís's father had asked Eduardo's mother to hide the baseball glove for him so that Luís's mother wouldn't return it because it cost so much. It wasn't *his* fault that all Eduardo had gotten for Christmas was a shirt, plus a book of prayers, plus three pairs of gray BVDs that were too big, as if they'd been bought for his older brother years ago and forgotten until this year—oh, and a harmonica that was missing three notes.

He sighed and tried again. "Want me to pump up the tires?"

Eduardo grunted, looking up at him. "Suit yourself."

By the time the tires were filled, Eduardo had loosened the nut and raised the seat. Now he couldn't tighten the nut.

"Wrap tinfoil on it, make the nut bigger . . ."

Eduardo gave Luís a sour look, but clapped rust from his hands and headed for the kitchen.

Luís stared at the spot in the dirt floor where Eduardo buried his money. How much money had Eduardo squirreled away? Enough to buy the glove from Luís? But how could he sell a present from his father? Jeez! The glove was ruining his friendship with Eduardo—and he hadn't even wanted it!

Eduardo came back and wrapped a scrap of tinfoil onto the nut, squishing it down tight. He picked up the wrench.

"Hey!" He sounded surprised when the nut moved.

Luís was relieved. "Take it out for a spin? I'll pedal." Luís didn't want Eduardo's mood to darken. Eduardo nodded and climbed aboard.

Eduardo bounced on the seat, testing it, as Luís tried to build up some speed. Up ahead, an ambulance turned the corner, siren screaming, and sped away. Luís stood, stomping on the pedals. "Follow?" he shouted over his shoulder. He'd always wanted to see a dead person.

"Yeah!" Eduardo shouted back.

Luís's heart pulsed like the ambulance light. When the ambulance disappeared around a corner, Luís followed its sound, turning from one block to another, until he didn't know if he was hearing the siren or just imagining it. Too winded to continue, he let the bike coast.

"Almost—got it," Eduardo said, puffing as if he'd been pedaling.

Luís was about to stop when he saw, coming toward them on the sidewalk, a man who looked like a movie star. The rolling walk, the eyebrows buttoned together, the way he carried his chin . . . "That Mickey Rooney?" he asked over his shoulder.

"Naw," Eduardo said for both of them, as they passed the guy. "Mouth's wrong. Hair too."

"Yeah," Luís said, his legs ready to collapse from chasing the ambulance. He pedaled once, to straighten out his other leg, and felt the front tire slowly sink into the pavement. He looked and saw that it was nearly flat. "Ah, ma-a-an!" He brought the pedals around to brake.

"Remember passing a filling station?" Luís asked as he and Eduardo stared at the tire. He hoped they hadn't strayed into Lincoln Heights.

Eduardo shook his head and spat, aiming to the side but hitting his own shoe. "*Pinche* bike!"

"There's gotta be one around here somewhere." Luís wheeled the bike down the block.

They came to an intersection and spotted the flying red horse of a Mobil station to their left, a couple blocks down. They galloped toward the sign.

Laying the bike near the air pump, they started toward the office. A man came out, hands on his hips. Each blond hair of his crew cut shone, making his head look like a light bulb. The cigarette dangling from his lips glowed like a filament.

"Howdy." The cigarette bobbed.

Luís pointed to the air pump and the bike. "Could we—may we put some air in our tires?"

A second man walked out and stood by the first man. His overalls were black with grease.

"What d'you say, Harv?" the first man asked. "We have any air to spare?"

"Depends. What d'you say, Ray?"

"Depends on if they want new air 'r old air—hot air 'r cold air—or air from New York City." Both men grinned.

Before Luís or Eduardo could say anything, a gray deSoto drove up to the pumps, making bells ring inside the office. A white-gloved woman tapped her horn.

"Mrs. Gerzon," groaned the man named Harv, moments before a green Chevrolet drove in, making the bells ring again. "You two know how to wash windshields?" Luís and Eduardo nodded and Harv handed them two rags he'd pulled from his back pocket.

"Squeegees over there," Ray said. He nodded toward Eduardo. "You get Gerzon." He looked at Luís. "Get the other feller."

Luís struggled to scrub off the bugs, which were hard as dried snot. He didn't look at the man inside, but he felt his stares. Was he watching to make sure the button of his jeans didn't scratch the paint? The man pointed from inside. Luís went over that spot again. The man nodded to dismiss him.

As the cars drove off, Ray sighed and took Luís's rag. "Guy said you did a nice job."

Harv nodded as he took Eduardo's rag. "Gerzon said the same—which is sayin' a mouthful for her. Know how t'use it?" He jerked his thumb toward the air pump.

"Yes . . . sir," Eduardo said.

"You boys got names?" Ray asked.

The spoke at the same time: "Luís." "Eduardo."

"You Mexicans?"

"Cut it out, Ray. They can't help where they was born, any more'n you can help bein' a Kraut."

Ray grunted. "You know we been lookin' for weekend help with the pumps, Harv. An' I don't know nobody works harder than a Mexican."

It was Harv's turn to grunt. "You boys like to give 'er a try?"

"Sure!" Eduardo's smile was the biggest in weeks.

"Yeah!" This was Luís's chance to *really* be the man of the house! Maybe they'd even get to work in the shop.

Ray handed the rags back. "Do good this afternoon and we'll give ya two bits each and invite ya t'come back. We'll split tips four ways."

If Luís and Eduardo had nodded any harder, their heads might have fallen off.

CHAPTER SEVEN

"*What* did you say?" Eduardo stopped and faced Luís, blocking the sidewalk.

"We're movin' to New Mexico—in a couple days."

"Why the hell you doing *that*?"

"My grandfather. He's sick, maybe dyin', and my momma wants to be there if, you know . . . to help."

"So. *She* can go, and while he's croaking, you can stay *here*. You can have Fernando's old bed."

Luís shook his head. Even if he could stay, he'd hate sleeping in Fernando's bed. It still smelled of cigarette smoke and Cinco Rosas hair tonic and a cologne that might have come from a whiskey bottle.

"Let my momma talk to yours, *ese*. And now that we got jobs, what can your momma say? Look. We each made thirty-four cents yesterday!"

Luís walked around Eduardo. "We're gonna be late."

Eduardo tucked in next to him. "Know what? I think you *want* to go to Mexico!"

"You gotta be kidding! And it's *New* Mexico," Luís said.

"Oh, right. *New* Mexico." Eduardo's voice was turning nasty. "What makes it so *new,* anyway? They breathe the air first, before it goes to *old* Mexico? Does everybody got *new* cars? Does everybody got *new* houses? Huh?"

"How should I know?" They began running at the sound of the church bell.

They looked for a place to sit together. But since the war had geared up, church was more crowded with each passing week, mostly with women whose husbands and boyfriends were gone. Eduardo grabbed the first spot, toward the back. Luís found a place halfway to the front.

Without Eduardo next to him, Luís found himself relaxed in church, enjoying Mass instead of worrying what his friend would think or say. He said the true words in response to Father O'Higgins, and he listened, liking what he heard.

Luís had always found it hard to describe his own feelings. Lately, words slid around whatever he felt: sadness, happiness, anger, fear, pride. As he listened to Father O'Higgins and the rustle of starched cloth, as he smelled the perfume of the woman next to him, as he watched patches of colored light shimmer on Christ and the altar, he imagined that the church itself held all his feelings at once, made them beautiful and comfortable together.

Luís imagined himself as a priest, living and working in church, at peace with himself and the world. Luís sometimes talked to God. But imagine—God talking back!

Imagine being a priest and having conversations with God, all chummy, like old friends! Luís was almost sorry when Mass ended. He looked for Eduardo as he shuffled through the front doors. He couldn't see him anywhere. Luís felt both relieved and miffed that Eduardo hadn't included him in his plans.

Luís found his mother in her bedroom, packing his father's clothes into a cardboard suitcase.

"Hi, honey," she said, looking up.

"Papa's clothes staying here, or going?"

"I don't know. He doesn't have that many, so maybe I'll just take them."

"But we're coming back, right? When your father's OK?"

His mother sighed. "I don't know when we're coming back."

"Why you acting like we aren't?" The peaceful feeling from Mass was fast disappearing.

"You *still* don't understand, do you."

"All I know is we're going where you grew up, where everything's perfect, where I won't find nothing like the gas station job in a million years!"

"Las Manos isn't perfect," his mother replied, surprisingly calm in her anger. "But—" Her face froze. "What did you say about a job?"

Luís hadn't meant for it to slip out. When his mother

told him last night that they were leaving, he'd forgotten all about the job. When he remembered, he decided to punish her by keeping it secret. "Some guys at a filling station want me and Eduardo to work for them on weekends," he said. "I thought we could use the money."

His mother sat on the bed and patted the spot next to her. He hesitated and then sat. "I'm sorry, Luís, it's more than your grandfather. And it's more than your father being gone. And it would take more than a weekend job to keep us from going. You see, I left my family in anger, and it's time to go home. It's time to mend things a little, to let you meet your grandparents and your other relatives." She reached for his hand. "I never thought I'd say this. But I'm looking forward to going home."

Luís pulled his hand away. All he could think was that she was going to take him to a place where the chickens were smarter than the people.

In all her fussing around, Luís's mother almost forgot the Christmas cactus. "I hate to leave it, Luís. But we can't take it with us on the train. Eduardo's mother can take care of it." He nodded.

Luís knocked on the kitchen screen door, cradling the plant in the crook of his other arm.

Eduardo's mother appeared, scowling, wiping her hands on a dishcloth. Her face softened when she saw him. "Luís. *¡Dios mío!* Come in! Why are you knocking? You're not *un hobo!*" She pushed the door open.

"My momma was wondering—could you take care of this while we're gone?"

"*¡Claro que sí!*" She took it, placing it next to the one above the sink. "Maybe yours will teach mine when to flower!" She chuckled. "Last year mine had flowers on Good Friday!"

"Where's Eduardo?" he asked.

"In his *cuarto.*"

As he walked down the hall, Luís wondered why Eduardo would be in his bedroom in the middle of a Sunday afternoon instead of playing baseball.

The door was ajar. Luís pushed it open. Eduardo was lying on his back in bed, elbows cocked like angel wings, his hands behind his head. At the sight of the door opening, he flew upward, sitting.

"Jeez," he hissed. "Thought you were my papa, wanting to yell at me again."

"Yeah?" He sat on Fernando's old bed.

"Somebody told my papa that I snuck outta Mass."

Luís knew this day would come. "Who?"

Eduardo shrugged. "Still going? To New Mexico?"

Luís nodded.

"Damn." Eduardo looked past Luís, out the window. "You'll forget me, you know."

"What d'you mean?" Luís asked, hurt and surprised.

"Won't take long, and you won't think about me no more. It'll be like we weren't never friends or nothin'."

"How can a guy forget his best friend?"

Eduardo shrugged again. "Maybe if you have some-thing to remember me by—" He stood on his bed and reached for the crucifix. Dropping to his knees, he held it out to Luís.

Luís hesitated. "I don't have nothin' for you, *ese.*"

Eduardo shrugged again and tossed it to him. Luís almost fumbled the catch. "You don't got one and I hate havin' Him stare at me all the time, anyway, lookin' so sad. Jesus—He's everywhere in this house—even in the bath-room!" He smiled. "Just don't do nothin' bad while He's watching. Do, and your nuts'll fall off."

"How d'you know, *ese*? Yours already fall off?"

From the other end of the house came Eduardo's father's voice. "Eduardo! Edua-a-ardo! *Eduardo!*"

Eduardo's face soured. "Jeez. Hide that thing!"

Luís stuck it down the back of his jeans and turned to face the door.

Eduardo's father appeared, making the doorway look skinny. He glared into the room. "I got paint and brushes." He disappeared.

"What's going on?"

"Gotta paint the shed," Eduardo said. "Punishment."

Luís shook his head. "I'll help, *ese.*" Eduardo seldom looked so surprised. "And you better not forget it."

PART TWO

LAS MANOS

CHAPTER EIGHT

Luís didn't want to look out the window of the train, but he couldn't help himself. Since plunging down the mountain from Canjon Pass to Barstow, what he saw outside was something out of a nightmare.

The ground itself looked like a rotting carcass, with wounds where the sunset's reddish light shone. Luís wouldn't have been surprised to see bones poking through the taut, leathery hills.

The growing darkness made a mirror of the glass. The landscape slowly cooled to ash colors, then faded, and finally disappeared. Before long all he saw was his own face, floating, bleary as gasoline on water. When the lights in the car dimmed, his face disappeared too.

Luís touched the ten-dollar bill his mother had pinned under the lining of his jacket, in case they got separated or she got mugged. Having it made him feel rich as a banker. He hoped his mother would forget about the money when they got to Las Manos.

He glanced at her and saw she was dozing. She'd been quiet the whole trip, as if her mind were in Las Manos already, waiting for her body to catch up. He checked his shirt pocket for the gum a soldier had given him that morning at Union Station. The place had been lousy with strutting soldiers, acting like pachucos but not dressed as well. They walked as if they had broom handles up their backs, the ends clamped in their butt cheeks, holding them in place.

He'd searched for his father among the soldiers. Maybe he'd gotten his mother's letter in time to hurry back from boot camp to stop them from going. Luís had been disappointed.

The gum was still there. But before he took it out, he had some business to take care of.

He edged around his mother and walked toward the back of the car. He felt unsteady, as if he were allowing the train to move under him when he lifted his feet.

He knew he'd found the men's room when he smelled cigar smoke. He stopped just shy of a doorway, from which words seemed to be rolling off glowing waves of smoke and, like the smoke, melting into darkness before he understood them.

The voices stopped when he entered the room.

"Hello." It was Percy, their Negro porter, sitting between two white men, one with a silver pocket flask in his hand. "Can I do anything for you and your mother?"

"Toilets?"

"In there." Percy nodded toward a dark wooden door.

The bathroom was a wonder of waxed wood paneling and of shining brass and painfully white tiles. Luís walked into the stall, undid his pants, and perched. The train's rocking made him nervous—he didn't want water sloshing onto his bottom.

Hitching up his pants, he wondered what would happen when he flushed. Was everything dumped onto the tracks? Or was it carried to some kind of tank? Pulling the lever, he bent as close to the roaring as he dared. But his head cast a shadow over the whirling water and he couldn't tell if it was emptied onto the tracks or not.

Luís brought the smell of cigars back to his seat. He took out the gum and smelled it before sliding off the paper and unwrapping the foil. It was fresh, coiling without crumbling.

Cold air coming from the window and the mindless, tasteless chewing soon made him drowsy. The train rocked him toward his mother. He barely had the strength to take the gum out of his mouth before falling asleep.

Luís woke with a start as his mother leaned him toward the window. "Keep sleeping," she whispered. "I'll be back soon."

It was too light to go back to sleep, and people were talking. Luís yawned and glanced out the window. Seeing snow on the ground jolted him awake.

He'd never been this close to snow, and it made the landscape appear strange and wonderful. When the glare of the snow became unbearable, he looked across the aisle.

The hills out the opposite window were brown, practically bare. Astonished, he turned to his own window.

Why was there snow on one side and not the other?

His mother plopped down beside him. "We're in New Mexico!"

"How come those hills have snow and those don't?" He pointed right and then left.

His mother smiled. "The sun melts the snow it touches on the south-facing slopes. On the north, where the sun doesn't shine, the snow stays."

"Oh." His eyes bounced from one side to the other, amazed at how different they were.

"Let's eat." His mother slid a basket from under her seat.

The bread of his sandwich was soggy with carrot water that had seeped into the waxed paper from a canning jar with a seal that had been used too often. As he ate, he watched the snow thinning outside. In a blink, like the second reel of a movie started too soon, the snow disappeared. He found himself staring at hillsides with dirt of different colors, some layers blue, some red, and some yellow.

When they stopped in the town of Gallup, an old man who looked like an Indian in the movies shuffled past the aisle, necklaces dangling from his hands, some sky blue and others silver.

When they'd started again, his mother squeezed his forearm and pointed out the window. "Lava fields," she said. What Luís saw looked like new scabs oozing from cracks in old scabs.

The stop in Albuquerque was a long one. Some passengers had other trains to catch, and new people came aboard. Three stops later they pulled into Lamy. A few people got off to take the spur line to Santa Fe.

"Las Vegas is coming up, where we get out." She began gathering their things.

Luís was tired of the train—tired of sitting and looking out the window, of rocking back and forth, of stale air and the smell of picnic food going bad. Even so, part of him wished it would take forever to get to Las Vegas.

Forever came quickly.

Percy, the porter, helped his mother onto the station platform. "Thanks." She handed him a dollar. A dollar! Luís could hardly believe she'd given him so much.

"Why, thank *you*, ma'am," he said, smiling.

As the train whistle blew, his mother turned to Luís. "Do you still have that ten-dollar bill?"

He hadn't checked for a while. His hand jumped to his jacket. "Yes," he said with relief. She reached up into the lining of his jacket and fumbled with the pin, the tops of her knuckles tickling against his ribs. But he couldn't laugh—he was too disappointed that his mother had remembered.

CHAPTER NINE

Luís stared after the train. The farther away it got, the more it looked like the tab of a giant zipper pulling the rails together.

"Maybe they're waiting on the other side." His mother sounded lost.

They lugged their things through the station. Dropping his suitcases, Luís studied the street in front of him.

Where was the "new" in New Mexico? He saw a man riding a horse down the street. Old cars and battered trucks wove around wagons pulled by horses. A boy led a donkey that was piled with firewood. His mother preferred *this* to Los Angeles?

And then she cried out, "Here! Here! *Here* we are!"

She waved at a dirt-colored truck. Its windows were so varnished with grime that Luís couldn't see the driver.

The truck ground to a halt, still shuddering as a tall, thin man leapt out.

"Solomón!" his mother cried.

"*¡Bienvenido!* Welcome!" The man lifted Luís's mother off the ground. "Sorry I'm late!"

"*¡Gracias a Dios!*"

His mother was speaking Spanish? Whenever he'd spoken it back home she'd gotten angry, telling him he wasn't a Mexican and shouldn't talk like one.

"Sarah!" He turned toward Luís. Around this man's neck was a priest's collar.

"You must be Luís," he said, reaching out to shake his hand. "And you must wonder who I am and where you are and when you can board the next train for Los Angeles. I'm your Uncle Solomón."

Luís could only stare, his head bobbing along with his hand. His mother's brother was a priest?

"Let me help with these." His uncle walked toward their luggage.

Luís hesitated. How was he supposed to act in front of this man? Was he more priest or more uncle? Did being a priest take turns with being an uncle?

His uncle grabbed two suitcases and Luís rushed to get the other two.

"Is this the Sandovals' truck?" his mother asked.

"Yes." His uncle threw the suitcases in the truck's bed and walked around to the passenger side. "And it used more prayers than gasoline to get here." He opened the door and let Luís climb aboard before helping Luís's mother.

Luís settled into the middle of the seat, his legs straddling the gearshift. He perched on the edge so he could see out the windshield.

The springs groaned as his uncle climbed in. "I hope it wants to get home as much as I do."

His mother was hugging herself, as if trying to keep from shivering. His uncle slammed the gearshift into low gear and took off. Luís scooted back a little, glad the gearshift hadn't slammed into his crotch.

His mother leaned over Luís and shouted above the engine's roar. "How's *Papí*? As bad as your letter said?"

Uncle Solomón nodded. "He has more bad days than good, and the bad days are worse. His heart is worn out. And we don't know if he's deaf or just pretending."

"How much longer are you able to stay here?" his mother shouted.

"Another week."

The road straightened, empty of everything but potholes. As they picked up speed, the rearview mirror shook so much it seemed to reflect everything at once. "How does it look to you, our *Nuevo México?*"

Luís squinted through the windshield. Before he could say anything, his mother shouted back. "*¡Qué lindo!*" It was hard for Luís to get used to his mother speaking Spanish.

The road began to wind as they left town, separating the foothills from the yellow plains that spread out on their right like a dead lawn. The steering wheel snapped back and forth, squeaking and groaning as if the truck were hitting squirrels and dogs and cats instead of bumps on the road.

64

"You think I'm doing the right thing, coming home?" his mother shouted.

Luís frowned. They'd left Los Angeles, traveled through a nightmarish land, and his mother didn't know if it was the right thing to do?

His uncle's answer was even more disturbing. "I don't know. There are still bad feelings about you leaving."

"We can go back, you know," Luís said, but not loud enough for anybody to hear above the rattling and roaring of the truck.

Luís didn't realize he'd been sleeping on his own shoulder until the quiet woke him. He lifted his head and stared out the windshield.

They were parked in front of a mud-caked house that seemed to be sinking into the ground under the weight of heavy shadows. The windows were trimmed in a blue that, in the falling darkness, almost matched the red of the strings of red chilis hanging under the porch.

"This is where I grew up," his mother said quietly.

Luís could see why his mother had left. It looked like some of the abandoned houses by the railyard where hobos slept.

"We'll get your things later," his uncle said.

Inside, the house was cavelike and chilly. Laid across the ceiling were long, naked logs. The lengths of split wood that spanned these logs seemed unnaturally dark, as if oily shadows had soaked into them night after night, day after day.

The plank floors were almost as dark, covered here and there with woven rugs, the edges rough as those on a postage stamp. Only the walls were pale, barely white enough to separate the darkness of the ceiling from the darkness of the floor.

His mother disappeared into a doorway that glowed yellow.

"Sarah!" came a voice like that of an old lady in church. "*¡Estás aquí!*"

Moments later, out rushed a woman no taller than Luís but much wider. "Luís?" She stopped in front of him, her eyes roaming his face. "Luís!" Her hug almost knocked him over.

When his grandmother stepped back, she grabbed his arm. "*Ven acá,*" she said, pulling him into the kitchen.

There he saw his mother kneeling in front of an over-stuffed chair in which an old man sat. The chair was close to a large wood stove that was so hot Luís felt its heat from the doorway. Even so, the man wore a hat and overcoat.

His mother stood slowly. "*Papí,*" she said, gesturing toward Luís, speaking loudly and carefully. "This is my son, Luís," she said. And then, as if correcting herself, she repeated, "*Esto es mi hijo, Luís.*"

Luís saw confusion on the old man's face. "*Como yo—otra vez,*" the old man said in a hoarse whisper.

His mother nodded. "Yes," she said softly, looking at Luís. "Like you all over again."

CHAPTER TEN

Uncle Solomón leaned toward Luís. "Let's go feed the chickens," he whispered.

Luís followed his uncle out the kitchen door, grateful to escape his grandfather's confused gaze.

The sky looked smoky but the air smelled clean. They walked toward a large, leafless tree. Around the tree was a fence made of branches poked into the ground and lashed together. Inside, chickens milled around a shed under the tree, in which two chickens were roosting.

"Do kids in Los Angeles play baseball?" Uncle Solomón reached for a stick propped against a covered barrel by the gate.

"Sure." Was his uncle making fun?

Uncle Solomón pointed. "Put some grain from the barrel in that pan and I'll show you how I learned to bat."

Luís scooped grain and tossed pinches of it in front of him. The hens in the tree leapt off the branch, landing with the grace of cannonballs in an explosion of dirt and feathers. A dozen hens swarmed, pecking at everything, including each other.

"Here he comes!" Uncle Solomón crouched, bringing the bat up in readiness.

A rooster came plowing through the hens, beating its wings, its neck fluffed up. It sprang, clawed feet aimed for Uncle Solomón, who crouched lower, and then slowly, almost gently, swung. The rooster flew backward, looping once before landing.

"Fowl ball!" Uncle Solomón cried, crouching again, the stick ready. The bird charged again, only to fly backward. The rooster took a few wobbly steps and began pecking hens as if they were to blame for what had just happened to him.

His uncle rested the stick on his shoulder, grinning. "He'll behave for now. Just don't turn your back on him."

Luís scattered more grain, stepping back as a hen pecked the top of a shoe. "They always this stupid?" He remembered his father saying chickens were smarter than the people of Las Manos.

"Yep. And roosters are stupid *and* mean. When I learned to hit a baseball, I'd picture a rooster coming at me and think how much it'd hurt if I missed." He grinned. "Time to get 'em in."

His grandmother was lighting candles in the pantry when Luís and his uncle stepped inside. The flames danced as she whispered to them.

Was his grandmother crazy?

"What's she doing?"

"She always prays at dusk on Friday," his uncle replied.

"Why?" But his uncle was at the kitchen table and either didn't hear his question or was ignoring it.

Luís sat next to his mother. His grandfather sat at the far end, still wearing his hat. The only sound in the kitchen was the occasional shifting of wood in the stove. Luís's back grew rigid in the silence. He began to breathe easier when his grandmother came from the pantry with food for the table. Only after his grandfather began eating did anyone else lift a fork.

The meal was mostly silent. Whenever his grandfather cleared his throat, which he did often, all eyes looked to him, as if he were about to say something. He never did, and nobody else seemed comfortable starting a conversation without him.

After dinner, as he helped his uncle fetch luggage, Luís learned that he was sharing a bedroom with his uncle. It had been his grandparents' bedroom, but they both slept in the kitchen, close to the stove's heat.

After getting his mother's luggage, Luís lingered in her bedroom, feeling shy about settling in with his uncle. He'd never shared a bed with a stranger before and it made him feel even more awkward to think that this stranger was his uncle and a priest. Could priests hear and see people's dreams? Luís had been having dreams lately even he, himself, was embarrassed to remember.

"This was my room when I was a girl," his mother

said, looking up at him as she sat on the bed. "Well, mine and Juanita's." She saw the puzzled look on his face. "My sister," she explained.

"Hasn't changed, has it?" Uncle Solomón asked, walking in, putting his arm around Luís's shoulder. "And still the coldest room in the house."

Luís's mother nodded. "Yes. But I remember on the coldest nights Juanita and I would drag you in here. We'd put you between us, to keep us warm." She sat on the bed.

Uncle Solomón laughed. "When *I* got cold, I'd sneak in the dog and make him sleep with me. That worked OK, except in the spring I got fleas."

His mother laughed. "Wasn't that the spring you fell in love with Audra Gallegos?"

Uncle Solomón nodded. "I was too embarrassed to tell anybody about the fleas, but I couldn't stop itching. I'm sure that's what scared her off." He smiled. "Just think. If it weren't for fleas, I might have married her and never become a priest. Not only God but fleas, too, work in mysterious ways."

"What happened to Audra?" his mother asked.

"She married Narciso Chacón."

"Narciso? I haven't thought of him for such a long time."

"Forgotten the time *you* tried to marry him?"

Luís looked at his mother in surprise.

His mother blushed. "Of course I remember. I was

70

ten or eleven and I just wanted to get it over with, marrying him. I was sick and tired of everybody telling me that my parents and his parents had already arranged for us to get married. And I talked you into performing the ceremony. Even then we knew you were going to be a priest."

"What a wedding! Instead of kissing the bride, Narciso slugged you in the stomach!"

His mother laughed. "Priests don't usually give the groom a bloody nose. Is Narciso still here—in Las Manos?"

"Yes," Uncle Solomón said, "and no. He's here, but in the *camposanto*. He died three years ago. A horse kicked him in the head in the rooster pull on Santiago's feast day."

His mother put a hand to her mouth. "And Audra?"

"She takes care of their five children and lives with her parents."

"Her father's still alive?"

Uncle Solomón nodded. "He used to come visiting. But not so much since *Papí* got sick."

"*Papí*'s worse than I thought," his mother said softly. "I thought I could help make him well again."

"He needed to see you, before he dies. To see you and his grandson."

"Can anything be done?" His uncle shook his head and his mother bowed hers. Luís didn't want to see his mother cry. Besides, he had things to unpack.

He turned and was startled to see his grandmother

just inside the doorway. The heavy cloth of her nightgown was the same color as her face, which was the same color as the walls. She looked as if she were a ghost stepping from the plaster.

"Hello, Grandmother," he managed to say.

"*¡Mamá!*" His mother jumped from the bed.

"*El viejo—*" his grandmother began.

Uncle Solomón held up a hand to keep his sister from rushing out the door. "She just needs help getting *Papí* ready for bed. Luís and I will take care of him while you get settled."

Luís was willing to help, but there wasn't much he could do except stand next to his grandmother and watch as his uncle helped his grandfather take off his hat and over-coat and pull a nightshirt over his shirt and trousers. His uncle worked carefully and skillfully, reaching under the nightshirt to undo and pull down his grandfather's trousers. Uncle Solomón nodded politely whenever his grandmother said something in Spanish, her voice worried, her hand flut-tering. His grandfather didn't resist any of this, but he didn't do much to help either.

When his uncle reached for a large ceramic pot near the bed, his grandmother shooed both of them away.

"Chamber pot," his uncle explained without being asked. "Your grandfather is too weak to go to the outhouse. But I have to go and I bet you do too. Let's see if your mother would like to come with us."

It seemed strange having company to take care of such personal business—especially when the company was his mother and uncle.

Outside, Luís couldn't keep his eyes off the stars. He'd never seen so many before. Even with the moonlight and light from the lantern his uncle carried, they were thick as spilled salt. His eyes stung as he looked up, as if the cold air was peppered with stardust.

"You first," his uncle said, handing him the lantern. There was no door. Luís stepped inside, not knowing if he'd be able to do his duty with his mother and uncle standing outside and with the half moon peeking in at him through the doorway.

The lantern's light flared in the stink of the outhouse. He peered down the hole, feeling the same unsteadiness as when he'd looked into the train's toliet. If it hadn't been for the cold, and his mother and uncle talking outside as they waited, he wouldn't have been so quick to sit over the hole's darkness.

The bed was lumpy, with a sag in the middle. Luís held himself rigid to keep from sliding toward his uncle. Every time he moved, sounds from the bed made him think he was disturbing mice in the mattress. His uncle was breathing heavily, and he could make out snores from the kitchen. His grandparents took turns snoring, as if they were having a conversation in their sleep. He would have preferred the rumbling of cars back in Los Angeles, or the occasional voices of people as they walked by at night.

Getting ready for bed, his uncle hadn't been at all embarrassed about undressing. He'd taken off his shirt and collar and was stepping from his pants before Luís could turn his back. Luís caught sight of a butt cheek. His uncle didn't wear underpants! What did it look like for a priest to be missing his nuts? Luís wasn't curious enough to peek at his naked uncle.

"You'll want to wear more than undies and a T-shirt," Uncle Solomón said, when Luís felt it was safe to turn back. He held out a pair of pajamas that were made of the same brown flannel he was wearing. "Here," his uncle had said. "They'll be big. But warm."

And then there had been prayers. Uncle Solomón knelt toward the foot of the bed and Luís followed his lead, kneeling toward the head of the bed. He couldn't make out much of what his uncle was mumbling, head bowed, hands clasped in front of him. His uncle's forehead was wrinkled in concentration.

Luís was out of practice. He bowed his head, clasped his hands, and frowned—just like his uncle. He finished quickly but, not wanting his uncle to think badly of him, he continued to mumble nothing in particular until his uncle sighed, "In the name of the Father, Son, and Holy Ghost" and crossed himself as he stood.

"God bless you," his uncle had said, reaching out and

touching Luís's forehead with his thumb. "And kick me if I hog too much of the bed."

Remembering these things, Luís lay next to his uncle trying not to move even though one leg of the pajama bottom was twisted, cutting into the inside of his thigh. When he couldn't stand it any longer, he began slowly to move a hand down to straighten it out and scratch the itch away.

Slowly, slowly, slowly his hand moved and then froze, when, from outside the bedroom, came a howling— a crying—a singing—something ghostly and mournful, electric as an air-raid siren.

It stopped.

Luís's hands flew up as he clutched his pillow. He slid into his uncle, who groaned.

The sound came again, closer to the house this time.

His uncle stirred and rolled onto his back.

Luís fought an urge to grab his uncle's hand. "What *is* that?" he managed to ask.

Right on cue the sound came again, but farther away.

His uncle reached for Luís's hand. "It scared you?" his uncle asked.

Luís nodded, his whole body shaking.

"It used to scare me too. When I was a boy my mother told me it was La Llorona, the ghost woman who walks along the *acequia,* the irrigation ditch, crying for her dead children. 'Don't play near the *acequia,*' Momma would say, 'or La Llorona will grab you. And if you're not one of her children, she'll throw you in and you'll drown!'"

"How did her children die?" Luís spoke in a hush.

"She drowned them herself, in the *acequia*."

"Oh." Luís shuddered. "Why?"

"When her husband ran off with a younger woman, she blamed them and their noise and the way they made her too tired to be a good wife. But when she came to her senses, she jumped in after them. She drowned, of course. But it was only a story. My mother told it to keep us from playing near water. It worked too, even when we learned it was just coyotes howling."

"Coyotes?"

"Yes. Like dogs, only wild." Uncle Solomón squeezed his hand and let go. "Go back to sleep, Luís. It's been a long day."

This time, Luís let the bed take him where it wanted. He felt safe being close to his uncle—his back resting on his uncle's back. He let his uncle's steady, deep breathing rock him to sleep.

CHAPTER ELEVEN

Luís tensed his shoulder against being shaken. Why was his uncle waking him when it was still dark?

"Luís!" came Uncle Solomón's voice. "Time to gather eggs."

Luís sat up so fast he nearly knocked heads with his uncle. He wasn't at home. He was in New Mexico. All the dreams he'd been having flew like bats from his head, into the dark.

"Meet you in the kitchen," Uncle Solomón said. "Don't forget your *cute*."

"*¿Cute?*"

"Jacket," his uncle replied.

His uncle was sitting with his mother and grandmother at the kitchen table. His grandfather was still in bed, tucked under the shadow cast by the stove. Luís made a face as he sniffed the air. "Something burning?"

"No," said Uncle Solomón, lifting his coffee cup. "You smell this. Toasted acorns, ground with a few coffee beans." He took a sip. "Coffee costs money. Acorns are free."

"Come here, Luís," his mother said. He walked to

her, his head bowed, knowing she was going to lick her fingers and comb his hair with them. He hated that—she might as well spit on his head and rub it in—but he knew better than to argue.

It was a shock going from the hot kitchen to the cold outdoors. The air hurt his lungs and his scalp tingled where his mother had dampened it. Inside the fence, Luís and his uncle waded through a puddle of darkness that was thick as water.

The stench in the shed blinded him more than the darkness and burned his lungs more than the cold. Slowly, a row of blurry white shapes began to appear.

"Be gentle as you reach for eggs." His uncle thrust a basket handle into his hand. "You start here."

Reaching under the first hen felt like what he imagined it was like under a girl's dress. Still holding the egg, he crossed himself for such a thought.

The first two chickens didn't mind his hand, but the third one clucked. Luís remembered the rooster and was more careful as he worked his way toward the middle.

Once outside, he breathed deeply, not caring how much the cold hurt. The sun had risen, its light scouring the landcape, replacing shadows with a scratchy grayness the color of dried soap film. Chickens poured from the shed, spilling like suds into the chicken yard.

As they stepped from the yard, an angry-proud-joyful cry came from behind. Uncle Solomón closed the gate just as the rooster flew into it.

"Know why roosters are so mean?"

Luís shook his head.

"Because hens have bigger *huevos* than they do."

Luís stared. Was he talking about eggs or testicles— or both? Were priests allowed to joke like that?

Uncle Solomón laughed. "Does God have a sense of humor?"

Luís had never thought about it before. "Got me."

"Sure He does!" His uncle tossed him an egg. Luís didn't have time to think of missing.

"That's how I learned to catch. You miss, you make a mess. You don't catch it right, it breaks in your hand."

Luís nodded and tossed it back, pleased to see surprise on his uncle's face.

Back in the kitchen, his grandfather was at the table, staring into his coffee cup. Again, everybody was quiet. Breakfast was *atole,* cornmeal mixed in hot water. Luís didn't like its sandy feel in his mouth or the way it sat in his stomach, but it took the edge off his hunger.

When the dishes were cleared, his grandmother spoke to his uncle in Spanish, squinting at Luís each time she took a breath. Was he in trouble already?

His uncle nodded and turned to him. "From now on, she wants you to fetch water every morning after you gather eggs. I'll show you."

Carrying a bucket in each hand, Luís followed his uncle to a well. What was he going to be here? A slave to his grandmother?

Next his grandmother wanted *leña,* so Uncle Solomón showed him where the firewood was stacked.

"We should split more," Uncle Solomón said after their second trip inside. He showed Luís what to do, handed him the ax, and stood aside.

It was harder than Uncle Solomón made it look. Luís was grateful when Uncle Solomón motioned for him to sit on the chopping block, big as a tire, and almost as black.

"You just need practice," his uncle said, "to build muscles in your arm as hard as that muscle in your head." He winked.

Luís nodded and looked at the pile of wood he'd chopped. Next to it was a bigger mound of adobe with a doorway carved into it.

"That a doghouse?" he asked, pointing.

His uncle laughed. "No. That's an *horno,* an oven for baking bread and cakes. You build a fire inside, heat it up, scrape out the coals, and put in the bread. When you close up the opening, everything stays nice and hot inside." He got up and brushed off the front of his pants. "Time for us to go inside, where it's nice and hot."

When Luís tried to stand, his pants seemed glued to the wood.

"Sticky?"

Luís nodded, pulling free. He looked where he'd been sitting. "What was that? Somebody's gum?" He checked the seat of his pants.

"No. Chicken blood. That's where we chop off their heads."

Luís toted yet another load of wood into the kitchen. His grandmother was knitting as his mother wrote a letter. His grandfather was in bed, sleeping.

"*¿Tienen hambre?*" his grandmother asked, looking up.

"*Claro que sí.* Yes, we're hungry," Uncle Solomón replied for both of them.

Setting her knitting on the table, Luís's grandmother went to some shelves by the stove. From a jar, she pulled something that looked like bark.

"*Carne seca,*" she said, smiling, handing him a piece.

"Dried meat," his uncle translated.

"*Gracias.*" Luís hoped it tasted better than it looked. He gnawed off a piece. Saltiness mixed with the bite of red chili powder. It grew larger as it softened in his mouth, like chewing gum come to life.

"Would you mail this?" his mother asked.

"Anything to keep from doing more chores." Uncle Solomón grinned. "Besides, I should return the truck."

With hands in the pockets of his *cute,* Luís looked ahead as he sat in the truck. Where was Las Manos? Where were the people? The cars? Bungalows and tenements? Sidewalks?

Luís searched for anything that would remind him of Los Angeles. They passed a clump of prickly pear cactus. Unlike the ones back home, these were scrawny and small, their spines looking like splinters of soggy wood.

Not only were the prickly pears scrawny and small but all the trees he saw were short and raggedy. Patches of snow, like white shadows, mirrored their shapes on the ground. Luís found himself longing for palm trees, their tall, smooth trunks swooping up to little skirts of dried leaves that twitched in the breeze, like girls walking.

They came to a larger road that curved left through a notch in the flank of a long, low hill. Once through the notch, they shimmied toward a cluster of buildings. The buildings looked as if the ground had shifted under them, leaning one against another. "Las Manos?" he shouted.

"Yep," his uncle replied.

The Japs would be crazy to attack this town, Luís thought. It already looked bombed.

The road threaded between two buildings, coming out into a square surrounded by more buildings. In front of the buildings was a dirt road, on which a couple pickups and a car were parked. Two horses and a burro were tethered to one side, heads down, kissing dirt. Opposite the horses was a well, its bucket raised.

Luís eyed small kids playing on the sunny side of the square. They stared as he and his uncle drove toward a store, its fake wooden front rising above the mud houses on either side.

A bell rang when they opened the door, but its sound was overwhelmed by the creaking of the wooden floor.

The store smelled dusty. Shelves filled with cans, tools, bolts of cloth, guns, and jars of candy lined the walls. Above hung animal heads—a deer, two bears, and a buffalo that looked like a nickel come to life.

Luís and his uncle walked to the back, toward a wooden Indian holding cigars and a counter on which leaned a balding man with a shiny head and cheeks to match.

"*¿Cómo está, Padre?* How are you, Father?"

"*Bien.*" His uncle put a hand on Luís's shoulder. "Mr. Sandoval, my nephew, Luís, from Los Angeles."

Mr. Sandoval reached out a hand. "Welcome to Las Manos! I would'a known who you were without being told. You look just like your grandfather!"

"Thanks." Luís stood on tiptoe to shake.

"Thanks for the use of your truck."

"*De nada.* Don't mention it."

"We have a letter to mail." Uncle Solomón put the letter on the counter and dropped several coins on top of it.

"What luck!" Mr. Sandoval said. "I just got a couple letters for your family." He winked at Luís. "One's for you."

"Thanks," Luís said. He recognized his father's handwriting on both of them.

"*De nada.*"

"Any news?" Uncle Solomón asked.

"Not much, Padre," Mr. Sandoval said. "Except that Mr. Zellman'll be here on Tuesday."

"I haven't seen him in years!"

"On the way out," Mr. Sandoval said, looking at Luís, "help yourself to a piece of candy from one of those jars under the deer."

Luís rushed into the bedroom he shared with his uncle. Sitting on the bed, he ripped the letter open.

Dear Luís,

Hi. Yep, I'm off to fight that Hitler guy. I'm ready. I've been yelled at enough to last a lifetime. And there's nothing more dangerous than army chow. Ha ha.

Well, she did it. Took you to Las Manos. Bet not much has changed since your mother and I left. Bet it's still as pretty as ever and just as poor. Probably doesn't have electricity and I bet Mr. Sandoval still lets people borrow that same old truck I used to borrow when I was a kid. And bet it doesn't work any better now than it did then. Ha ha.

Guess you've figured out why we left by now. I always wanted to tell you, but your mother wanted to wait. If you have any questions, ask your uncle the priest, if he's still there. He's a good guy and shoots straight. We could use more of his kind in the army. Ha ha.

Golly, my hand is hurting from all this writing. Don't want to wear out my trigger finger!

Anyway, just want to tell you that I love you, son. Hope you're helping your mother. I miss you both very much. I'll write again when my hand has recovered. Ha ha. Give your mother a big old smacker for me.

Dad

Luís folded the letter and put it on the nightstand, noticing that Eduardo's crucifix was facing the wall. He turned it around. Why *had* his parents left? Was it because Las Manos was so poor it didn't even have electricity? Or toilets in the house? Or radios?

"Good news?" Luís looked up at his uncle, standing in the doorway. He nodded, even though he was disappointed his father had been too hurried or tired or shy to tell him what life in the army was really like.

"Time for *lonche.*"

In the kitchen, he startled himself and his mother by giving her a kiss. "From Dad," he explained, blushing.

CHAPTER TWELVE

"Uncle Solomón?" Luís and his uncle were walking to Mass. The sky was clear, but there was a cloud in Luís's head.

"Yes?"

"My crucifix keeps turning around, facing the wall."

Uncle Solomón smiled. "When I was a boy, my crucifix did that too. And then one day I caught my mother turning it toward the wall."

"Why'd she do that?"

"To punish Him, 'til He made life easier for her family."

"Punish *Christ?*"

Uncle Solomón nodded. "People around here sometimes punish the saints—even God!—when things go wrong. I know a family that buried a statue of the Christ Child to punish Him for letting one of their babies die. And then, the morning after the next baby was born, they found the hole opened up and the statue sitting in front of their fireplace. Nobody knew how it got there. Maybe Christ figured that they'd had another child, so His punishment was over."

"Is Grandmother turning the crucifix around to punish Christ for Grandpa?"

"Could be."

As they approached the notch in the hill, the sound of a bell drifted toward them. Uncle Solomón began to trot. Luís fell in beside him.

They slowed to a walk when they came out on the other side of Las Manos. Uncle Solomón was barely winded, and Luís struggled not to gasp for air. To their right was a field, sloping from the town, seemingly roped in place by an energetic creek. To his left were two buildings. One had a cross on a wooden bell tower.

Several people greeted Uncle Solomón as they drew near the church. All of them reached for Luís's hand after they shook his uncle's. By the time they entered the church, Luís had shaken at least a dozen hands. As Luís wiped his palm on his pants, he wondered if that was how Las Manos—The Hands—got its name.

There were no pews in the back half of the church, and all the pews in front were filled. Luís and his uncle stood.

Luís looked around as he waited for Mass to begin. Above the altar was a gruesome crucifix—gray, except for bright red blood that dripped into Christ's eyes and mouth from the crown of thorns. Christ's face was twisted in pain. More blood oozed from His palms, and from a gash in His ribs, and from His knees and feet. The crucifix back home was calm—more sad than pained—and bloodless.

When the music started, Luís was surprised to find himself listening to a guitar.

Luís followed Mass as best he could. He watched his uncle carefully for clues, glad to have a priest at his side. It was at once familiar and strange, like a song on the radio played too slow, the words Spanish instead of English. It didn't help that the priest's voice was higher than Father O'Higgins's. Most unnerving, each time Luís looked toward the altar, he saw one of the altar boys staring at him.

When Mass was over, people once more gathered around his uncle, speaking Spanish with English words thrown in. Once more Luís found himself shaking hand after hand.

A boy stepped up to him. He was tall and thin, his hair combed back and shining in the sun. "You Luís?" It was the altar boy who'd stared at him during Mass.

"Yeah."

The boy reached out a hand. "I'm Antonio." Luís felt calluses as he shook. By now other boys had gathered around.

"You really from Los Angeles?" Antonio asked.

Luís nodded.

"You picked oranges out your windows?"

Was this guy making fun? "Only when they were ripe." He watched to see if Antonio knew he was joking.

"*¡Increíble!*" The other boys murmured their wonder.

It *was* incredible. They believed him!

"You ever see movie stars?"

Part of Luís hated leading this guy on. But he couldn't resist. "Sure. Lots."

"Who?" asked a large boy with a blackened front tooth, his eyes growing big in spite of his efforts to frown.

Luís's mind raced. "Just the other day I saw Mickey Rooney."

"*¿De veras?*" Antonio asked.

Luís couldn't tell if he was curious or doubtful. "Sure. He was walking along the street and he had babes all over him. When he snapped his fingers, one would hand him a cigarette and another'd light it. He'd take a couple puffs and give it away."

This was *pinche* good! Luís was picturing it as if he had really happened. Imagine! Seeing Mickey Rooney!

A kid with a straw hat piped up. "How 'bout Betty Grable?"

"Sure," Luís answered. "Once I even saw Bette Davis buy makeup at the drugstore. And gum." Luís was afraid of pushing this too far, but he couldn't help himself. "And once I saw Rita Hayworth buying shoes. Must have cost a hundred bucks!"

"*¡Chingón!* Wow!" Antonio had a dreamy look on his face. "A hundred *dólares!*" And then he blinked, as if waking, and squinted. "You don't know who I am, do you?"

"Sure. You're Antonio."

89

"No. I mean, *sí*. I'm Antonio. But," he grinned, "I'm also your *tío*—your papa's youngest brother."

Luís stared. Was this guy getting back at him for pulling his leg about the oranges?

Luís felt a hand on his shoulder. "I see you've met your uncle Antonio," said Uncle Solomón. "How are you, Antonio?"

"*Bueno*, Father Naranjo."

"And your mother?"

"I am well," came a voice from behind.

Luís turned to the person who spoke, an old woman who looked like his father dressed up as an old woman. His father was a handsome man, but his grandmother was not a pretty woman. Her hair was white and her long dress was black. The skin of her face had the drippy look of wax that had melted and hardened.

"Señora Medrano!" Uncle Solomón held out his hand.

"Padre." Her smile was polite but hard as the rest of her face. And then she looked at Luís. "*¿Mi nieto?* My grandson?" Without waiting for an answer, she held out her hand to him. Was he supposed to shake it or kiss it? He shook.

"*Buenos días*," he said in his best Spanish. "*Abuela*."

"I speak English," she said, her accent heavy, "better, no doubt, than you speak Spanish. I am happy to meet you. How is your father?"

"Fine."

"And your mother?"

"She's fine too."

"And your mother's parents?"

Before Luís could answer, Uncle Solomón spoke. "They are well, Señora, and will be pleased you are well also."

"By the grace of God, Padre." And then, acting more like a queen than a grandmother, she turned to Antonio. "¿Listo?"

"Sí, Madre. I'm ready."

He held out the crook of his arm, and she took it.

Uncle Solomón looked at them walking away. "Old wounds heal slowly."

"Wounds?"

"Your parents never told you?"

Luís shook his head.

Uncle Solomón took a deep breath. "When your parents wanted to get married, your father's mother and father were reluctant, but they finally agreed. My parents, however, wouldn't give their approval. You see, they'd already arranged for your mother to marry Narciso Chacón. They always said, 'Marry for love, live in sorrow.' So when your father's older brother came to ask, they sent him home with three *calabazas*."

Luís looked at him in puzzlement.

"*Calabazas* are pumpkins. If a young girl's family

gives them to the boy's family, it's the same as saying 'no' to getting married. Your father's family was insulted, as if our family had told them your mother was too good for your father. It's a wound that still hasn't healed."

Uncle Solomón sighed. "What do you think of *la muchachada*?"

"The what?"

"The gang."

"My mom said there aren't any gangs in Las Manos."

Uncle Solomón laughed. "Not the same as in Los Angeles. But wherever there are two or more boys, there's usually a gang."

They started walking toward Las Manos.

Uncle Solomón turned to him. "Want to see the best place I know for you to pick raspberries this summer? Everybody's so busy with their crops when they're ripe that I don't think anybody knows about it. Except maybe bears. And you have to promise not to tell anyone—except maybe your uncle Antonio."

Luís grinned. "I promise."

CHAPTER THIRTEEN

———————◆———————

"Ready for your first day of school?" Uncle Solomón asked as Luís came in the kitchen carrying the basketful of eggs he'd collected. Coffee with roasted acorns no longer smelled strange.

"Guess so."

His mother beckoned and, reluctantly, Luís walked toward her, his head bowed.

"Remember," his uncle said, "these kids have grown up together and they're pretty tight knit. But with Antonio being your uncle, you'll be all right."

When his mother was satisfied with his hair, his grandmother shuffled over with a cup of *atole,* which seemed to settle to his feet.

As Luís swallowed the last of the *atole,* Uncle Solomón got up from the table. "This once, I'll finish your chores. Go on. You don't want to be late."

It was strange walking to school with no other kids in sight. The first kids he saw were a handful of boys playing baseball in a field between the church and the school. One of them hit the ball high. Several large ravens circling overhead swooped toward the ball, but pulled away as it started down. A boy in center field stepped forward and caught it in his bare hands. Antonio. No wonder Luís had felt calluses yesterday when he shook his hand.

By the front stairs of the school, some littler kids were throwing pebbles at the upright backbone of a large animal leaned up against the wall, a flat rock barely balanced on top where the head should be.

Luís watched, trying to figure out the point of this game, until he heard the thump of approaching footsteps. "That's *hueso*," said Antonio, barely panting from his run. "A game for babies. You play baseball?"

Several boys had followed Antonio. "Sure," Luís said.

"Any good?" asked the large boy with a blackened tooth.

"I'm OK." Luís didn't like the doubt he saw in the boy's face. "I got a glove."

Antonio's eyebrows shot up.

"I'm not *that* good," Luís said. But he saw in their faces that his modesty was proof to them that he really was good.

The large boy with the black tooth held out a hand. "I'm called Raul."

"I'm called Ubaldo," said the boy with the straw hat. Luís shook their hands—and the hands of Jorge (who looked as if he hadn't shaved this morning), Rudolfo, Alejandro, and Sabine (who spit tobacco toward the kids playing *hueso*).

94

A blond woman stepped from the school, ringing a hand bell. She smiled as Luís walked past her. "Wait for me by my desk."

Inside, there was only one large room. Luís had heard about such schools before—like the kind Abraham Lincoln had gone to, back when a penny had been worth a quarter now. Girls sat on one side, boys on the other. Young kids were in front. In the middle of the boys' side sat Antonio, Raul, Rudolfo, and Alejandro. In back of them were Sabine and Jorge.

Luís waited, watching the teacher, liking the way she talked to the kids as they came in. Once behind her desk, she opened a grade book, the pages puckered with writing.

"I'm Miss Woodward." She spoke in a way that told him she thought he might have trouble with English. "What is your name?"

"Luís Medrano." He liked the way she wrote his name.

"And where are you from, Luís?"

"Los Angeles. In California."

"How lovely," she said. "I've always wanted to visit the City of Angels." She peered into the classroom. "Please sit there." She pointed toward Antonio and Raul. She smiled. "Welcome to Las Manos, Luís!"

When Luís sat, Antonio leaned over and whispered, "She's new. From Chicago. And she don't *habla español*. You know, speak Spanish."

Everything about this school was different, except for

95

the Pledge of Allegiance. Hand on his heart, Luís glanced at the girls. Just like in Los Angeles, he saw that their hearts must shift when they grew titties.

How did anybody learn anything with everybody doing different things? The room buzzed like a badly tuned radio as kids worked in pairs. Miss Woodward reminded Luís of Eduardo's mother tending several pots on her stove, never letting anything boil over, adding salt here or chili powder there.

Miss Woodward may not have been able to speak Spanish, but she understood it. When a little girl asked her questions in Spanish, she answered before reminding her to speak English.

"Please read the first two stories in this book." She handed Luís a *McGuffey's Reader* on her way to Sabine and Jorge, who were laughing none too quietly. They didn't laugh long.

He tried to read but couldn't concentrate. It was a great relief when Miss Woodward announced recess.

Antonio walked with him to where a burro was hobbled. Sabine was leaning against it. All the boys gathered around.

"Catch." Without warning, Sabine tossed something to him. Surprised, Luís caught it with one hand.

The ball was made of glossy brown leather. It felt small and had flattened corners where it should have been round. Luís weighed it in his hand. It seemed a little heavy.

Rudolfo grinned. "Nice, eh? Sabine made it from the testicle of a goat. And he made this bat from his *abuela's* wooden leg." Rudolfo handed Luís a bat that looked as if it had been made from a table leg. It was sanded and rounded, nicely balanced, and about the right weight.

"Don't listen to him," Antonio said. "He's got *basura* for brains. You know, garbage."

Sabine glared as he took the bat from Luís. "I'll hit. The rest of you go out and catch."

Luís walked between Antonio and Ubaldo toward right field. Just before they got set, Sabine yelled, "*¡Velís!* Heads up!" and hit. The ball flew between Luís and Ubaldo in center field.

"Yours!" Luís called. Ubaldo snagged it on the first bounce.

"*Gracias,*" Ubaldo said, and then corrected himself. "Thanks."

"That's OK," Luís said. "*Hablo español, un poquito.*"

"*Sí,*" Ubaldo replied, grunting as he threw the ball to Sabine. "You speak Spanish like a Mexican."

Luís was about to tell Ubaldo he wasn't Mexican when he heard the sound of bat against ball. It reminded him of an overripe orange hitting the side of somebody's house. As the ball grew larger, Luís realized it was coming toward him.

He stepped back, reached out, and watched it land at his feet.

Luís picked it up. Had he looked as stupid as he'd felt?

"It's not really a testicle," Raul called from left field, sounding serious.

Luís threw the ball to Sabine and readied himself, but the ball didn't come at him again before Miss Woodward rang the bell.

Antonio walked to him. "You'll get used to our ball. And maybe tomorrow you can bring your glove and show us a thing or two."

"Maybe." Luís cursed himself for mentioning the glove.

"Having a bad day?"

Luís looked at Sabine and shrugged. Sabine smiled, but not in a friendly way, and spit tobacco as they came to the school steps. "Tomorrow, I got something for you that'll help."

"Watch out for that Jew," Antonio whispered, letting Sabine go up the stairs first. "He don't like your family. Or mine."

Luís followed Antonio, thinking the people of Las Manos had a weird sense of humor. How could a Jew look like a Mexican?

Without being asked, Luís fetched water and wood for his grandmother and then rushed to the chicken yard. When Luís opened the gate, the rooster let out a cry that seemed to loosen the feathers around its neck and attacked. Luís grabbed the stick by the barrel.

He swung, hoping he wasn't being too gentle. The stick stayed in his hands as the bird expertly pushed off with his feet, sailed backward, and landed on top of a hen. Again the rooster flew toward him, this time curving in from the left. Luís stepped back and swung more firmly but not too hard, connecting.

When he connected a third time (low and inside), Luís remembered what the pachuco had said across from the Evergreen Cemetery: "Make 'em pitch it where *you* want it."

It had sounded like good advice at the time. But how could you make a rooster pitch itself where you wanted?

The rooster attacked twice more. Twice more Luís connected. He was disappointed when the rooster began running around the yard, pecking hens. It was the best he'd ever batted, and he didn't want to stop.

CHAPTER FOURTEEN

"Don't forget!" his mother called as he walked outside. "We're buying shoes after school at Mr. Sandoval's!"

"I won't!" Luís called back.

It was sunny and cold, and Luís was glad for the warmth of the baseball glove on his left hand. He tried to take his mind off the cold by trying to imagine the buildings and apartments of Los Angeles, surrounded by palm trees on the bare hills around him.

As Luís entered the plaza, he saw Antonio run from a house in the far corner. "Hi!" he called, wondering if that was where his father had grown up.

Antonio trotted toward him. "You brought it!"

Luís nodded and handed over the glove.

"¡Chingón!" Antonio stroked it. "Can I try it on?"

"Sure."

"Haven't played with it much, have you?"

"No." Luís took a deep breath. "I'm not that good at baseball," he blurted. "Just 'cause a guy has a glove doesn't mean he's good, y'know."

"Wasn't the ball any good?" When Luís shook his head, Antonio took off the glove. "Like my Uncle Cleo.

He's got the fastest horse around, but he don't win no races." He handed the glove back. "The horse, he's so fast, Uncle Cleo always falls off before the finish line!"

Luís smiled, relieved, wanting to get something else off his chest. "Know what else? I couldn't pick oranges from my window."

"I knew that." But the look on Antonio's face told him differently. "Mickey Rooney—that was true?"

Luís didn't want to disappoint Antonio more than he already had. "Yeah. And about Rita Hayworth too."

"¡Chingón!" Antonio smiled.

At school, everybody wanted to try on the glove. Just as Raul was handing it to Ubaldo, Sabine rode up on his burro.

"Look at this!" Ubaldo said, holding out the glove.

Sabine hobbled his burro before taking it. "It's softer than a priest's hand!" he said with scorn. "Not like this." He held out his own palm, its calluses looking thick and shiny as fingernails.

"Ah, come on," Antonio said. "You're jealous."

Sabine shrugged. "Mira. Look," he said to Luís, digging around in his pocket. "Yesterday I told you I got something to help you play better." He pulled out a closed hand. "What you need is some of this medicina." He opened his hand to show a half-dozen white pellets, like pills but fuzzy. Sabine tipped the pills into Luís's palm.

They were surprisingly light. "This is medicine?"

101

Sabine nodded. "They'll work better than that glove. But don't chew. They don't work good if you chew."

Luís looked at the other boys, wondering what to do. Everyone's face was blank. What if they would make him sick? Would anybody try to stop him?

Luís picked one up and brought it toward his mouth. Why was everybody staring at him? The thought of putting the pill in his mouth made him queasy, but he kept bringing it closer. Would they think less of him if he chickened out? Just as he opened his mouth, Antonio hit his hand. The pill went flying.

"Don't."

"What you doing, *cabrón!*" Sabine shouted.

"You've had your *fon*," Antonio told him. He turned to Luís. "I didn't think you'd fall for it." He sounded disappointed. "Those're nothin' but deer droppings, covered with lime."

Luís saw the sweat in his palm had stripped off some of the lime and had brought out a musty smell, not unlike mouse turds. He'd almost eaten a deer dropping!

At the sound of Miss Woodward's bell, the *muchachada* moved toward the school.

"Why'd he do that?" Luís asked Antonio, shaking the droppings from his hand as they walked toward the school.

"Like I said, his family don't like your family. Or mine."

"Why?"

"His father was supposed to marry your mother. And then your mother ran off with my brother."

"His father was Narciso Chacón? The one who died?"

Antonio nodded.

If things had worked as the families had planned, Sabine would have had Luís's mother for a mother. Did that make him, Luís, related to Sabine in some way?

The day went quickly. Miss Woodward praised his reading and writing and liked how he multiplied and divided. Luís had always been a good student, but Miss Woodward made him feel like a genius when she asked him to help a boy named Francisco with his handwriting. Luís had never used a slate before, and the chalk's grit scratched letters over thousands of other letters already etched into the tablet.

At recess he shared the glove with everyone, and he didn't make a fool of himself even once. Maybe just holding the "pills" had worked a little, and the joke was on Sabine and not on him, Luís. After lunch he practiced hitting with the other boys. He hit two out of three pitches and got beaned only once. Eduardo would have been proud.

That afternoon he read on his own and helped a girl named Angela add columns of numbers. And then— bingo!—school was over.

"Wanna help with my chores?" Antonio asked as they walked toward Las Manos.

Luís shook his head. "Can't. Gotta get shoes at Sandoval's store."

"Don't worry. While your momma's waiting, Mr. Zellman'll be selling shoes to the wooden Indian and telling stories so funny she'll forget you aren't there."

Luís smiled as they walked into the plaza. "Sorry," he said. "Good try, though. I got my own chores to do. After."

Antonio grinned back, nodding. "Just don't let the Jew sell you two left shoes." He looked up at the mountains and sniffed the air. "Smells like snow." He looked down. "Better go. See you mañana!"

Luís rushed into the store and found his mother and uncle by the back counter, sitting on chairs. Between them, on a stack of boxes, sat a man in a hat and a white beard. They all looked so serious. Was something wrong? And where was Mr. Sandoval?

"Hi." He studied his mother. What was she thinking about?

"Come here," she said, trying to smile. "I want you to meet Mr. Zellman. He used to sell me shoes when I was a girl."

The man in the hat stood. "You must be Luís." He reached out a hand. "We were just talking about you."

"Pleased to meet you, sir." Solemnly, Luís shook Mr. Zellman's hand.

Mr. Zellman dropped Luís's hand and smiled. "Come, come! What's with the long face? I don't sell shoes to horses!"

Luís was relieved when Uncle Solomón laughed. "I'm glad to hear you joking, Mr. Zellman," his uncle said. "I was beginning to wonder what happened to the man who could sell three shoes to a yardstick because it has three feet!"

Mr. Zellman shook his head and then clapped his hands. "Step back, Luís! Let me look at those hooves of yours!"

Luís stepped back.

"You're about my granddaughter's age." Mr. Zellman sounded so certain, Luís nodded before wondering how old she was. "And you wear a six—in a D width." He stood and pulled a box from where he'd been sitting. "Let's see how this fits." He sat Luís in a chair by his uncle and opened the box. The shoes inside were like those worn by all the boys in Las Manos: brown with a leather cap on the toe and a neck that went over the ankles. They were ugly but looked as sturdy as the soldiers' boots Luís had seen at Union Station.

As Mr. Zellman laced the new shoes, he glanced at Luís. "I think you'd like my granddaughter. She's from the big city too. Kansas City. Last summer, when she visited, she wanted to plant carrots on the flat roof of our house. 'Why?' I asked. 'Because,' she said, 'they'll grow down through cracks in the ceiling already sliced. And we can pull them without having to go outside.'"

Luís smiled and the store filled with laughter.

When the shoe popped on, the pain made Luís remember the time Eduardo ran over his foot with the bike.

"Stand," Mr. Zellman commanded. Luís stood, and Mr. Zellman poked at the shoe. Luís couldn't feel the poking. "Wiggle your big toe!" Luís tried, but the shoe gripped it too hard. "Nice," said Mr. Zellman. "And room to grow! I'll lace up the other, see if your feet are the same!" When Luís stood again, Mr. Zellman pronounced them perfect.

"How much, Mr. Zellman?" his mother asked.

"For you, two-fifty."

Uncle Solomón handed Mr. Zellman silver dollars and change.

"I'll put your old shoes in the box," Mr. Zellman said.

Luís's feet were in trouble before they crossed the plaza. He tried to ignore the cramping as he listened to his mother and uncle.

"I've never seen Mr. Zellman so sad," Uncle Solomón said. "What he said about Europe! Things must be worse for Jews there than we know."

His mother nodded. "The woman I worked for tried to get her parents out of Germany. After Pearl Harbor, she couldn't."

"It's a dangerous time for Jews," Uncle Solomón said.

They walked the rest of the way in silence, Luís trying to keep his mind off the pain in his feet.

"Where's the smoke—from the chimney?" his mother suddenly asked as they came within sight of the house. She turned to Luís. "Did you fill the woodbin this morning?"

"Yes. And I fetched water too."

"It's probably nothing to worry about, Sarah," his uncle said over his shoulder, sounding worried as he trotted toward the house.

Luís tried to keep up with his uncle and mother. As he hobbled into the kitchen, he was surprised to find himself alone. His grandfather's bed was empty, the covers pulled over onto the floor opposite the stove, and Luís could see his panting breath.

His breathing froze as a wail filled the house, sounding like that of a coyote, coming from the bedrooms. Had a pack of coyotes broken into the house and killed his grandparents? Was his mother being attacked? His uncle?

Luís grabbed a knife from above the stove and rushed to his grandparents' bedroom, ready for anything except what he saw.

On the bed lay his grandfather, face up, eyes and mouth open, his skin the color of the sheets. His grandmother was curled up on her side, clutching the old man's arm.

"Aiee-yee!" It didn't seem possible that his grandmother could make such a sound.

"Momma!" His mother reached out a shaking hand and touched his grandmother, who shuddered. Howling filled the room again.

Uncle Solomón passed a hand over his father's eyes, closing them. "Leave her there," he said to his sister. "Sit beside her. Comfort her. I'll make a fire in the stove and go tell Jacobo and his family that we need their help. Come with me, Luís." Uncle Solomón took the knife from his hand. "There's nothing we can do except bring in more wood. And I must borrow Mr. Sandoval's truck to tell your aunt Juanita."

Luís walked toward the woodpile, so numb he didn't feel the cold or the pain of his new shoes. His grandfather was dead—and he, Luís, had finally seen a dead body. It wasn't anything like what he'd imagined.

CHAPTER FIFTEEN

Luís thought he was batting at a moth until it landed on his cheek and melted, becoming a cold tear that ran to the corner of his mouth. Snowflakes came down harder as he and his uncle walked down the road.

"Looks like a storm's coming." His uncle reached for his hand.

As fast as Luís walked, his uncle pulled him along faster. "I've given many people their last rites, but it was different with my own father."

"You gave him last rites?" Luís had always thought of last rites as something to make up for last wrongs. It sometimes worried him to think he might die without them and go to hell.

Luís saw the pain in his uncle's eyes. "He made me promise that I wouldn't. But I'm a priest and I made a promise to God first. I gave him last rites while he was sleeping, two nights ago. It was the best I could do."

"Why didn't he want 'em?"

Snow gathered on his uncle's eyebrows. "You don't know, do you?"

"Know what?"

Uncle Solomón's grip became uncomfortably tight. "We're Jews, Luís. *Judíos.*"

Melted snow had dribbled into his ears and he shook his head. "Wha'd you say?"

"We're Jews," his uncle repeated, louder.

How could his uncle tease at a time like this?

"You don't believe me."

Why was his uncle pushing? "It's not funny." Luís tried to pull his hand from his uncle's. His uncle held tighter.

"You don't believe me."

"Look, it's not funny!" Luís shouted. "Don't joke like that! 'Course we're not Jews. And leggo my hand!"

"I'm not joking," his uncle said quietly, letting go. "We *are* Jews, Luís. It's something our family's kept secret for hundreds of years because—because it's always been dangerous to be a Jew—and not just now with Hitler. It's a secret we kept even when your mother ran off to marry somebody who was not from a family we share this secret with. Now—now you must promise to keep our family's secret."

It was an even crueler joke that his uncle wasn't joking.

"Sometimes," his uncle continued, "the biggest secret of all is that there aren't secrets in a town like Las Manos. When I was a boy some kids would get angry and call me *judío* or *matador de Cristo*. They didn't know what it meant, any more than I did, but somebody had told them."

His uncle turned onto a side road. "I know what you're feeling, Luís. When my father told me, he took me to the river and scooped water in his hands and poured it over my head, telling me I was unbaptized. For the first time, I almost hit him. I yelled, telling him I was going to be a priest. I told him I'd pray for his soul. He laughed. 'Good,' he said. He said that if I became a priest people might stop talking about us. But people didn't."

"I don't wanna be no Jew!"

"You know what, Luís? Christ was a Jew. When I think back, I knew all along that our family was different from our neighbors. Think about it, Luís. Just like Jews, we don't eat pork. I was always told it would make me sick. And there's more. We slaughter our own sheep and cattle in our own way. And, just like Jews, we don't drink or eat the blood they spill. We even wash the blood off meat before we cook it. We've never gone to the trouble to eat fish on Friday, and my father always wore a hat—even in church. And, like Jews, we've always circumcised our boys."

"Nobody did that to mine!" he shouted, picturing Adam's pecker. Did his uncle's look like that? And his grandfather's?

Luís saw squares of light ahead. As they approached a long, low house, his uncle said, "This family is one of us.

Son judíos." He knocked on the door. When it opened, Luís found himself looking into Sabine's face.

"I must speak with your grandfather," Uncle Solomón said.

Sabine led them to a parlor and disappeared.

A few moments later an old man walked into the room. "Solomón! What brings you here on a snowy night!"

"My father has died."

The man's face fell. "I'm truly sorry to hear this."

"I was hoping," Uncle Solomón said, "that your family could help my mother and sister—and sit with my father."

"*¡Claro que sí!* Of course!" The old man turned to Luís, as if seeing him for the first time.

"This is my nephew, Luís," said Uncle Solomón.

The old man extended his hand. "The one from Los Angeles," he said.

Uncle Solomón turned to Luís. Were those tears, or melted snow dripping from his eyebrows? "Tell your mother," he said, "that I'll be back soon."

"Sabine," said the old man. "Fetch your coat. You must help with Luís's chores."

Luís waited in the parlor while Sabine fetched his coat. It was true, what Antonio had said about Sabine being a Jew? It was hard to believe. Sabine wasn't like any Jew he'd known in Los Angeles.

"Luís?"

He turned to see a woman about his mother's age standing in the doorway. She was dressed for the cold. "I'm Sabine's mother. We're ready."

Luís stared for a moment. This was the woman who'd married the man his mother had been promised to?

Outside, it was snowing so hard Luís was afraid of breathing in flakes. The snow appeared to glow, brightening the way.

Light shone from every window of his grandparents' house. A lamp hung under the portal, by the front door. They knocked snow off their shoes and let themselves in. Candles flickered everywhere, making the air waxy.

Luís led them to the kitchen. His mother turned from the stove. "Audra! You came!"

"Sarah!" Sabine's mother met her hug with one of her own. "How could I not come?"

Sabine's voice was gruff and low. "Let's do your chores."

As they walked outside, Sabine took a chunk of tobacco from his pocket and cut off a plug with a pocketknife. "Want some?" He sounded halfway friendly.

Luís shook his head. "What're they gonna do in there?"

"Say some mumbo jumbo while they wash your grandfather and dress him back up. He'll look like he's taking a nap."

Luís reached for the stick as he stepped into the gate.

Several white lumps fell from the tree's low branch. The snow seemed to come alive as chickens ran around, white against white.

With a war cry, the rooster charged. Without thinking, Luís crouched, the stick ready. He tapped the rooster, who sailed back into darkness. When it attacked again, Luís tapped him once more.

Sabine yelled over the din of panicked chickens. "*Pinche gallo.* Let's feed 'em and get 'em inside, before they freeze or coyotes get 'em."

Sabine's mother greeted them at the kitchen door. "Luís, you're wanted in the bedroom."

His grandfather lay on his back, dressed in a black suit, his arms folded over his chest. His grandmother sat on one side, holding his grandfather's arm. His mother sat on the other, hands in her lap.

His mother looked up as he walked in. "He was married in that suit. Only sickness made him thin enough to wear it again." She wiped her nose.

Luís sat next to his mother and stared at his grandfather's face. Unlike this morning, he was shaved. A flap of skin, where he'd been nicked by the razor, hadn't bled. His lips were thin and gray.

What was it like to be dead? Where was his grandfather's soul? Did Jews go to heaven?

A commotion in the kitchen interrupted his thoughts.

In the doorway stood a woman who looked like his mother, only puffier.

"Juanita!" His mother pulled herself around Luís's chair. After they'd hugged and cried, his mother beckoned to Luís. "Luís, this is your aunt Juanita."

"I am pleased to meet you," Aunt Juanita said, her English stiff. She made way for several people crowded behind her. "Let me introduce your uncle and cousins."

Her husband, Moisés, was tall and thin, one fuzzy eyebrow bridging his eyes. Her children, three girls and a boy, looked like versions of his aunt quickly painted by various artists, some of them not very good. Luís tried to see something—anything—in their faces that said they were Jews. He couldn't.

Uncle Solomón shouldered his way into the room. "I have coffee on." He looked at Luís. "Go rest. It'll be a long night. Let your aunt sit with your mother for a while."

Luís retreated to the bedroom he shared with his uncle. He sat on the edge of the bed. His feet ached and he unlaced his shoes. Had Junho felt like this, a Korean but called a Jap? How could he, Luís, look like a Mexican and be a Jew? It seemed impossible—like being a girl and a boy at the same time.

Luís reached toward the crucifix and, not feeling it, looked to see pieces of it scattered on the table by the bed.

Serves Him right! Luís thought. How could He have listened and watched, pretending to protect, when all the while He knew that Luís's family was Jewish? What had He thought, watching Luís going to catechism, enjoying church, even sometimes toying with the idea of becoming a priest?

He heard shuffling and turned toward the door, where his cousins were gathered. They looked miserable—too shy to come in and too curious to leave. Luís didn't want company, but he said, "Come in." They shuffled in, looking at everything in the room but him. After a few minutes their curiosity began to overwhelm their shyness.

"Could you pick oranges from inside your house?" asked the boy called Benjamín, glancing sideways at Luís.

Before Luís could answer, the girl named Roberta piped up. "You ever see movie stars?"

"Yes," he said, wondering how many times he could get away with this. "I picked oranges from inside my house all the time—but only when they were ripe. And I saw lots of movie stars. The place was lousy with 'em. Once I saw Mickey Rooney. He was walking down the sidewalk and he had babes all over him." Luís took a deep breath. His cousins' big eyes told him he could push this story to the moon.

When Luís and his cousins returned to the kitchen, it was filled with people talking quietly among themselves.

For the first time in his life, Luís stayed up all night, several times sitting by his grandmother as she held vigil over his grandfather. The greasy candlelight seemed to stain everything it touched.

Luís was relieved when morning came, suddenly and unexpectedly, the light bouncing off the snow, bright as headlights aimed through the window.

CHAPTER SIXTEEN

◆

Before his grandfather died, there had been moments when breathing the cold New Mexico air had felt like breathing in light. With each breath his thoughts had brightened. Breathing it now only filled his lungs with the vast emptiness of the sky and numbed his thoughts with its blueness.

Luís listened to the crunch of shoes on the frozen road as he and his uncle walked to the cemetery. The sound made him realize that, for the past few days, he'd felt as uncomfortable with his uncle's news as his feet had felt in their new shoes. But the shoes were breaking in, and so were his feelings. He still had blisters on his heels and an ache in his gut, but either he'd gotten used to the pain or the wounds were healing.

"You've been quiet the past few days," his uncle said. "Tell me what you're thinking."

"Not much," he said.

"Well," Uncle Solomón said, "I've been thinking. I'm sorry I told you about our Jewishness when I did. I should have let your mother tell you—or told you when I wasn't feeling the shock of my father's death."

"That's OK," Luís mumbled.

"But now that I've broken the egg," his uncle continued, "I don't want to waste it. So I think I should tell you a few more things."

Tell me it's not true! Luís wanted to cry. He certainly didn't want to hear any more secrets.

"For me, finding out about our family's Jewishness was especially hard because . . . well, your momma was right about me always wanting to be a priest. I don't suppose you can understand that, wanting to be a priest."

Luís kept looking ahead. "I've thought about it—a couple times."

"Really?" His uncle sounded surprised.

"Yeah." Luís hesitated. "I like church. The way it feels. What it makes me think about. You know—" He paused. "Why'd you want to be a priest?"

His uncle thought for a moment. "I wanted to make the world perfect. Not better. Perfect. I remember when I was eight, I went out to the chickens with a pan of water that—God forgive me!—I'd blessed. I baptized every single chicken. I nearly drowned a couple, but I believed the chickens would taste better, be more nourishing, and their eggs too, if their souls were free of sin." Uncle Solomón laughed.

"And when my father told me I was Jewish, I wanted to prove to him that Christ was the Messiah the Jews had been waiting for. I wanted to prove to him that I wasn't a Jew and that he wasn't either—that we were better than

Jews." He looked at Luís and smiled. "What a little rooster I was! When I studied for the priesthood, things jumped out at me, pointed a finger, and called me Jew! Each time that happened I'd go eat some bacon or I'd say a hundred Hail Marys. And then one day I read something that changed my thinking."

They passed the road to Sabine's house. "I was reading about the Inquisition in Spain, which happened in 1492."

"When Columbus sailed the ocean blue?" Luís blurted.

"Yes. And the year the king and queen ordered all Jews to leave Spain or die if they didn't become Christians. Some Jews were burned at the stake, just for show, and many left for Portugal or Holland or even Turkey and North Africa. I've often wondered what it was like for the Jews who stayed, what it was like for them to become Catholic—not because they believed but because it was the only way they could live where they grew up, keep the businesses and farms that their ancestors had created."

They came to the notch in the hill, with its tunnel of cold air. "I started to wonder what was thicker: blood or holy water? What d'you think?"

Luís shrugged. "I don't know," he answered, wondering if this was the kind of trick question Father O'Higgins liked to ask during catechism. He'd always heard that blood was thicker than water. But what if it wasn't thicker than holy water? All he knew was that holy water tasted nasty. Had it tasted nasty because he was a Jew?

Uncle Solomón continued. "Some Jews decided they could act like Christians in front of other people—go to church, baptize their children, even send a son or two off to become priests. But they could be Jews in their hearts, in secret. Families must have gathered secretly to read the Old Testament and to observe Jewish holidays. They risked death to do these things because they decided that blood was thicker than holy water."

As they came out of the notch, the air grew warm in the sunlight. "Some families jumped at the chance to go to the New World, first to Mexico and then to New Mexico, where it might be easier to be secret Jews."

"Our family was one of those families?"

His uncle nodded. "And Sabine's family and a few other families around. There are enough families like ours nearby that I'm told a Star of David was secretly carved in the floor of our church, under the altar."

"What's a Star of David?" Luís asked.

"A star with six points. It's a powerful symbol for Jews, named after a powerful king in the Old Testament."

Luís pictured the blue star his mother had made for his father, and the stained-glass window of the synagogue on Breen Street.

They walked through the plaza in silence, Luís lost in

his thoughts. Who would have guessed? A priest who was a Jew! It seemed crazy. They passed Mr. Sandoval's truck, parked in front of the store, ready to take Uncle Solomón that afternoon to the train station in Las Vegas. Did his uncle have a Jewish pecker? Wouldn't somebody check to make sure priests weren't Jews? Surely it was as obvious as not having nuts—or having them when he shouldn't. Was his uncle like other priests in this way?

"What's it like, being a priest?" Luís wasn't sure how to ask about what he really wanted to know.

"That's a difficult question, Luís. Why do you ask?"

Luís hesitated and then blurted, "What was it like when you became a priest and—and your nuts fell off?"

Uncle Solomón stopped and stared. "Where'd you hear *that*?"

"My friend Eduardo, back home."

"And you believed it?"

Luís blushed. "Well, yeah. When I asked him how he knew, he asked me if I'd ever seen a nun with boobs— as if that had anything to do with it. But it made sense, at the time."

His uncle shook his head in wonder, smiling as he began walking again. "Well, Luís. I've got testicles, all right." He winked at Luís. "I just don't think with them, the way some men do."

They walked toward the *camposanto,* toward the brown mound of Luís's grandfather's grave. It poked through the thinning snow that now looked like rotten cloth. The grave had no marker. His uncle had told him that it was the custom in their family to mark a grave only after a year passed. "I'll be back," Uncle Solomón had said, "in a year. With a marker." Luís was afraid to ask if this was a Jewish custom.

Luís held his uncle's hand and stared at the mound, wondering if worms cared whether a body was Jewish or Catholic. He pictured his grandfather wrapped in the shroud, looking like a cocoon ready to hatch a giant moth— or an angel.

Luís looked at his uncle's face. "Why didn't we bury him in a coffin?" he asked.

Uncle Solomón grunted. "It's been our familiy's custom for as long as anyone can remember. It might be something Jewish. But who knows? Sometimes, over time, the meanings get lost."

"Do Jews go to heaven?" Luís asked.

His uncle put an arm around his shoulder. "Christ was a Jew," he said, quietly. "And He went to heaven, didn't He?"

It sounded to Luís as if his uncle didn't know.

"Write often," his mother said, speaking over the rumble of Mr. Sandoval's truck. She kissed Uncle Solomón on the cheek and wiped a tear first from her own cheek and then from his.

123

"I will." He turned to Luís, reached into a pocket, and pulled out a silver dollar. "Here."

The coin almost covered Luís's palm. "Thanks," he said.

"Ready?" Mr. Sandoval called from the driver's seat. "Don't want to miss the train!"

Uncle Solomón climbed aboard and slammed the door. The truck's bouncing made his wave look like a sloppy sign of the cross.

His mother reached for his hand. She held it tightly as the truck disappeared, filling the plaza with a silence that echoed in Luís's heart.

"Hey, Luís!"

Luís and his mother looked across the plaza. Luís admired the way Antonio ran—his arms and legs loose, his feet springing from the ground.

Antonio stopped in front of them, barely breathing hard. *"Buenos días,"* he said, dipping his head to Luís's mother.

"Good afternoon, Antonio," she replied. "If I didn't know better, I'd have thought you were my husband, running across this plaza when we were young!"

Antonio smiled. "Any news from my brother?"

Luís and his mother had each received a letter the day his grandfather was buried. Luís's letter had been filled with jokes about how bad the army food was (so bad one of the guys had started barking one day and couldn't stop) and about a pal of his—a bachelor farmer from Iowa—who actually thought the food was good.

To Luís the letter sounded like his father was trying to cheer him up. What wasn't he telling? Luís was beginning to think that what people kept to themselves was more important than what they talked about.

"He's well," Luís's mother answered.

Antonio nodded. "My mother'll be pleased for the news."

"Tell your mother I'll visit soon, will you?"

"With pleasure," Antonio said.

"Luís," his mother said. "I must see how your grandmother's doing. Don't forget your chores."

Luís nodded. "I won't."

"It was good to see you, Antonio," she said, hurrying off.

"Wanna come see my cow?"

"Sure."

"We could run her around the pasture," Antonio said, "get her bag really shaking, so she'll give butter instead of milk. Best butter in the world."

Luís hesitated. "OK," he said, wondering if he was being tricked.

Antonio laughed, punching Luís in the shoulder. "City slicker! You can't make *mantequilla* like that!" Still smiling, he said. "Now you don't hafta feel bad about the oranges."

"Antonio! Luís! *Ven acá.*"

Antonio looked toward his mother, who was frowning as she stood at the front door. "She's gonna put us to work," he muttered.

But when they approached, she smiled. "Come inside." Tipping back her head, she aimed her gaze down her nose. "I made *bizcochitos.* And they're—*¿cómo se dice?*—hot!"

Inside, Antonio's house was very much like the Medrano's, except for the corner altar in the front room. Luís looked around with big eyes. This was where his father had grown up! And this woman had been his father's mother, even though he had a hard time imagining her as anything but a stiff grandmother, even with Antonio. In the kitchen, she sat the boys down at the table and brought over a plate heaped with cookies. Antonio seemed tense, as if he were a guest in his own home.

"Luís, I don't want a stranger for a grandson," his grandmother began. "Please, take a *bizcochito* and tell me about yourself." When he hesitated, she asked, "What was it like to live in *la Ciudad de los Angeles?*"

Antonio relaxed. "Tell her about the oranges," he said, winking. "And the movie stars."

Luís reached for a cookie. "Well—" he began.

How far could he push it with his grandmother? He saw in her eyes that he'd have to be careful.

126

CHAPTER SEVENTEEN

"Wanna take a break?" Antonio asked.

Luís's back ached, his arms were heavy, and his hands (even with their calluses) felt raw. But he kept hoeing in the *huerta,* chopping weeds between chili plants. "No," he said.

"Come on!"

Luís kept working. "Can't take it, *flojo?*"

"Your head *fracasada?* Been out in the sun too long?"

It was hot. The sun sucked up sweat as fast as it came from his skin, just as the earth sucked up water as fast as it flowed from the *acequia.*

"Go ahead. Take a break. Don't let me stop you."

"What's wrong with you?"

Luís threw down his hoe and laughed, hands on his hips.

Antonio wiped sweat (and anger) from his face with the back of his hand. "You *bribón.*" He smiled sheepishly. "Let's check the *compuertas.*"

They walked to the head of the field, where water bled from gates in the *acequia.* Right after Easter, Luís had helped the men and boys of Las Manos clean the ditches, including this one. Then he'd helped Uncle Moisés prepare the fields for planting corn, chili, and squash. Since then, he'd helped irrigate Antonio's family's fields and let Antonio help him in return.

More than corn and squash and chili had grown from all this work. Friendship too—between Antonio and Luís, between Luís and his father's mother, between Antonio and Luís's mother's mother. Two days ago, Luís had gone home for lunch alone to find that his grandmother had set a place for Antonio too. Yesterday Antonio's mother had called him *m'jito* instead of Luís as she fried slices of cheese with sugar sprinkled on top for lunch.

Luís helped Antonio slip the wooden slat into the *compuerta,* stanching the flow of water. They sat on the bank of the *acequia,* looking out over the fields and the town beyond. Luís remembered how ugly Las Manos had seemed to him when he first arrived. The constant comings and goings of people to and from the dirt buildings had reminded him of ants. Luís remembered spending hours tormenting ants in his backyard in Los Angeles—putting things in their way, poking at the hills, riling them, uncovering eggs.

Looking at Las Manos reminded him of all that, except, now, he was one of the ants.

The warmth of the sun and the whispering of water made Luís drowsy. "Finish?" he yawned. "Before we fall asleep?"

"Sure," Antonio said, standing. "But first—" He stepped backward into the *acequia* and sat in water up to his chest. "Ai-e-e-e-e!" he shouted.

Luís laughed and did the same. "Ai-e-e-e-e!" he yelped. The water came from melting snow in the mountains. He climbed out, freezing where he was wet, warm where the sun hit his head.

During the summer, after Mass, the *muchachada* gathered by the school for a few minutes of baseball. It was all the time for play any of them had. Because the boys were careful not to soil their Sunday clothes, it was a different kind of game than before. Luís looked forward to playing in these games.

Luís and Antonio rushed from the church. Luís wanted to hit the ball high enough to knock one of the circling ravens from the sky. He wanted to catch the ball with his toughened bare hands, to let somebody else play with the glove.

Raul puffed up his chest. "I'm gonna be riding in the *corrida del gallo* next week," he announced.

"No!" someone said.

"*Claro que sí.*" Raul smiled, showing his black tooth. "I been practicing with my horse."

Luís didn't know what Raul was talking about. All he knew was that next week was *el día de Santiago*, the holy day for Santiago, the patron saint of Spain and horses and conqueror of enemies of the church. It was the biggest celebration of the summer, even bigger than the Fourth of July, which had come and gone a few weeks ago with barely a mention.

"What's a *corrida del gallo*?" Luís asked.

Antonio looked embarrassed for him. "It's a little something that happens after Mass and the procession," he said. "Something before the *baile*, with all the dancing."

"And drinking *mula*," said Jorge, staggering a few steps from where he stood.

Luís couldn't help himself. "What's *mula*?"

Some of the boys laughed nervously.

"Corn liquor," Alejandro answered. "With a kick like a mule."

Luís nodded and listened to the boys talk about the fighting that came after the *mula*. When nobody made a move for the field, he waited for a break in the conversation and asked, "Wanna play some ball?"

"Who's playing music for *el baile*?" asked Ubaldo, ignoring his question.

"Probably El Greco—same as always," Raul answered.

The silence grew awkward. "Gotta go," Sabine finally said. He spit tobacco off to the side and then left.

Rudolfo cleared his throat. *"Pues,* me too." Other boys grunted in agreement.

Luís and Antonio were silent on their way home, until Luís asked, "A *corrida del gallo*—isn't that how Sabine's father died?"

Antonio nodded. "He was *boracho,* but that's not why. Everybody's a little drunk. No. Somebody forced beer down his horse's throat. And his horse was a worse drunk than he was."

"A drunk horse?" He'd never heard of such a thing.

"*Sí.* Sometimes people do that to other people's horses, to win a race or to make a horse fight other horses." He looked at Luís as they entered the plaza. "Help me with my grandmother's *milpa* tomorrow?"

"Sure," Luís answered, wondering if he'd ever know enough to feel at home in Las Manos, know enough not to ask stupid questions.

The week went by in a blur of hoeing and irrigating and gathering eggs and bringing in wood so his grand-mother and mother could bake bread and pies in the *horno* for the fiesta before the dance on *el día de Santiago.*

On Sunday, of all days, he overslept. His mother was too busy in the kitchen with his grandmother to notice this until they ran out of wood. By the time he'd brought enough wood inside it was almost too late for Mass.

Running toward the notched hill, he saw a sky so bright it seemed to be ringing, though the sound came from the church bell. As he popped out the other side of the notch, the bell stopped, but the sky continued to hum.

The church was packed. And hot. From where he stood by the door, puffs of air cooled his neck.

He couldn't see the altar, and he was too far back to

131

hear well. He knew Mass was over only when people began to move and talk. People in front of him pressed back against one another, making a path through which marched four men in white tunics with red sashes and shiny black boots that rose above their knees. One of them was Jorge, struggling not to smile.

As Luís stepped outside, these men appeared from behind the church on the backs of nervous horses, who had flags and wilting flowers tied to their bridles. The horses pranced in place, eyes wide and nostrils flared, as the statue of Santiago riding a horse came from the church, carried on a litter by four men, one of them Uncle Moisés. He tried not to think of his uncle's secret, not wanting to give it away.

The statue of Santiago was dressed in new clothes and riding a white wooden horse whose bridle was made of rosaries looped through a hole drilled through its carved and painted mouth. From under Santiago's helmet came clumps of reddish hair, which had been cut from Antonio's father's head when he was a boy. It had been dark then but had faded over the years, turning the red of Spanish nobility, people said. A miracle? Who knew.

In Santiago's uplifted hand was the sword he used to vanquish enemies of the church. Jews, perhaps? Luís watched the horsemen lead Santiago toward Las Manos, followed by the priest and a double line of men, women, and children. Many times, the horsemen galloped ahead of Santiago (as if clearing a path) and then swung back, passing along both sides of the procession. When Antonio came from the church, Luís tucked in beside him.

The procession entered the plaza and turned right, following the road. Chickens panicked at the sight of so many people surrounding them. Dogs barked and children left the procession, standing in the plaza's center to watch. Luís wanted to join them—the parade must have been more fun to watch than be in.

Around the plaza they went. By now the line had stretched, and when Luís and Antonio came out of the plaza, Santiago was disappearing into the church. The line bunched up outside, as if the doorway were clogged.

By the time they got back to the church, Luís saw horses and riders gathering near the school. Bottles were passed around, tipped high as men took slugs.

A few men began yipping like coyotes. Luís and Antonio joined the crowd gathering between the church and school.

"Who's got the roosters?" one of the horsemen shouted.

An old man appeared with a squawking basket and a short-handled shovel. Setting down the basket, he dug a hole in the ground, flipped off the basket's lid, and plunged his hand inside. Out came a thrashing rooster, which he thrust into the hole, pushing and pressing dirt around it. He spat as he stood, and the rooster strained to peck at the spittle but could barely move its head.

After much shouting and arguing, the horsemen split

into two groups that faced each other across the field. The rooster was between them, still struggling in its hole, still furious.

"*¡Al gallo!*" the old man cried, and a horseman from each team galloped toward the rooster, leaning from his horse, reaching. The crowd gasped as the men came toward each other, swerving apart at the last moment. Both men had gone past the rooster, which had tucked its head and become quiet. The men stood in their saddles, cursing, pulling on their reins.

"*¡Al gallo!*" the old man cried again. Luís held his breath when he saw one of the new riders was Raul, leaning so far his head almost touched the ground. The other rider leaned too far, falling off. The crowd gasped at the tangle of horse legs so close to the tumbling man's head. From the corner of his eyes, Luís saw Raul grab the rooster by the neck, pulling it from the ground.

The rooster didn't make a sound as it dangled from Raul's hand. He swung the bird around. "Ai-e-e-e!" he shouted.

Both sides charged, aimed for Raul and the rooster, kicking up clouds of dirt. The clouds collided, making it difficult to see what was going on. After a few moments, a rider (not Raul) shot from the clouds, holding the rooster high.

"Uncle Cleo!" Antonio shouted. Luís stared. The one who never won horse races?

Another man (Uncle Moisés?) grabbed the bird. Feathers seemed to explode as the men wrenched the bird one way and another. With a popping sound, the bird tore. Moisés held the head while Cleo held the feet and body. Galloping to the crowd, Cleo swung the body around, yelling and laughing. Blood flew and women and children screamed, covering their eyes with hands.

Antonio grinned toward Luís, blood splattered on his face and shirt. "The more blood, the more rain we'll get— the better the harvest'll be."

Luís nodded and looked at his own blood-flecked shirt. He licked his lips and tasted blood, and remembering what his uncle said about Jews not eating blood, he licked again.

"*¡Otro gallo!*" one of the horsemen bellowed. And once more Luís watched the old man bury a rooster up to its neck.

In waves, men rode until one grabbed the rooster, starting a free-for-all. Six more roosters followed. The third rooster was trampled by the horses before it could be pulled.

By the last rooster, the horses and men were tired. They went through the motions of fighting for the rooster, but their hearts weren't in it.

Shouting insults, boys and men from the crowd ran onto the field, chasing after the man with the rooster.

Alejandro passed Luís and Antonio and leapt onto the man's horse, grabbing the rooster, throwing it to

Antonio. Antonio missed, but he managed to kick it toward Luís, who held it to his chest and ran—where, he didn't know.

The pounding of a horse approached from behind. A hand grabbed the collar of his shirt, lifting him off the ground. "Give it here, *sapo!*"

Luís dropped it. The hand let go and he fell, face first, skidding across the ground.

Luís stood, blinking enough dirt from his eyes to watch the horses and men and boys crowd together between the church and school. He licked more blood from his lips, not knowing if it was rooster blood or his own. Didn't all blood taste the same—whether it came from chickens or pigs or Christ or Jews or even *pinche* Japs or Germans?

Yipping like a coyote, Luís ran toward the horses and the men and boys.

PART THREE

STAR-CROSSED

CHAPTER EIGHTEEN

Luís refused to sit by the window of the train. Instead, he stared sourly down the length of the car, feeling as if the train were digesting him, slowly as a snake. It was hard for him to believe he was headed back to Los Angeles.

How had it happened? One day he was full of plans to chop enough wood for winter and maybe get a puppy, maybe get a cow to milk, go hunting with Antonio in the fall for elk and deer, maybe learn how to butcher chickens and sheep from Uncle Moisés, sneak away with Antonio for a day and go skinny-dipping at a hot spring up toward the mountains. The next day he was helping his grandmother move her things to Aunt Juanita's and listening to his mother tell him they were moving back to Los Angeles.

"I've written Eduardo's mother. We'll stay with them until we find a place of our own, and I find a job. I want us to get settled before school starts."

Remembering this, Luís took a deep breath to calm himself. Instead of stale train air, he wished he were smelling piñon burning in the kitchen stove. Instead of the harsh *clickety-clack* of the train, he wished he were listening to the soft sound of wind through the trees and the haunting calls of coyotes as they ran through the hills. Already Luís missed Las Manos as much as he'd ever missed Los Angeles.

He'd argued with his mother and then, furious because he couldn't change her mind, he'd run all the way to Las Manos.

The ache of leaving Antonio had been terrible. He'd left behind not just a friend but an uncle who was more like the brother he'd never had. Luís had even sometimes thought of Antonio as a walking, talking version of his father as a boy.

"Maybe I can visit, come see movie stars," Antonio had said when Luís had choked out the bad news. "Or maybe you can come back next summer."

Luís had nodded. "I brought you this," he'd said, handing the baseball glove to Antonio.

Antonio had reached out and then snatched his hand away. "I can't take that!"

"Please. It means a lot to me to give it to you."

Reluctantly, but unable to keep from smiling, Antonio had taken the glove. "*Gracías*," he'd whispered.

These thoughts were interrupted by someone saying, "Blanket, sir? Blanket, ma'am?" It was Percy. When they'd boarded the train in Las Vegas this morning, Luís had been surprised to see that he was their conductor.

"Why, thank you," his mother said, taking one for Luís also.

"My pleasure."

Seeing Percy made Luís feel that he'd never left the train, that New Mexico had been nothing but a dream.

His mother's eyes were closed and her head rested on the window. He stared at her. Did she know that Uncle Solomón had told him the family secret? Not once during the summer had she brought it up, and he sure hadn't. Did she know that he didn't know if she knew that he knew? Secrets of secrets of secrets! Sometimes secrecy seemed more important than the secret itself! He frowned.

"Why are you staring at me?"

His mother opened her eyes.

Startled, Luís turned to look forward.

"Come on," she said, sitting up. "My eyes were open a crack. The way you were frowning made me feel like a bug."

"I thought you were asleep."

"Why were you frowning?"

And then it came out, just like that, without warning. "Why didn't you ever tell me before? 'Bout your family?"

She sucked in a breath. "How did you find out?"

"Uncle Solomón."

She nodded, sighing. "I wanted to. Many times. But I could never screw up my courage."

"Is that why you hardly ever go to Mass?"

She nodded again.

"And I'm not really allergic to pork?"

She shook her head. "But my family never ate it. We believed it was dirty meat."

"And that's why we didn't have crucifixes around our house?"

She nodded and then hugged him, kissing his forehead. "You're full of questions, aren't you? Don't be afraid to ask. I'll tell you what I can, but I don't know much."

Luís had plenty of questions. But right now he felt as if he'd chugged a bottle of soda, and that the fizz had gone to his head instead of his stomach.

The blanket warmed him, making him drowsy. When he awoke, the train was pulling into Union Station, its brakes sounding like huge knives being sharpened.

Luís flinched when cars and trucks passed as he and his mother lugged their suitcases down the sidewalk.

"What do you think of Los Angeles?" his mother asked, setting down her suitcase at a trolley stop.

"Don't know," he said. "Kinda loud. And smelly." The car and truck exhaust was giving him a headache.

"That's what I thought too, my first time here, fresh from Las Manos, and with a new husband." She laughed. "In our family we had a saying: 'If you come for the kisses, you must stay for the farts.'"

Luís was shocked, and his mother laughed gently at his wide eyes. "It came from our ancestors, and my grandmother would speak sayings like that in a strange, old language called Ladino. When I first came here, full of kisses for your father, the stinky Los Angeles air made that old saying pop into my head. I've never been able to get rid of it." A red trolley approached.

Luís helped his mother wrestle their luggage into the trolley. Looking out a window, it seemed to Luís that the sky had shrunk. With all the buildings crowded together, Luís felt as if he'd shrunk too.

Much of what he saw along Brooklyn Avenue looked vaguely familiar. It was as if somebody he hadn't seen for a long time had become taller and thinner, with shorter hair and a changed voice. Only when they crossed the bridge over the Los Angeles River did he know why everything was confusing. Where had all the Mexicans come from?

Luís was relieved to see that Eduardo's house looked the same as before. He and his mother walked around to the back.

"¡Dios mío!" Eduardo's mother cried, rushing to the door. Flour puffed through the screen as she pushed the door open. Her hands were white with flour but, keeping her hands by her ears and reaching her elbows out, she hugged Luís's mother anyway. "You're here!" Tears ran down her plump cheeks.

Luís looked around. The kitchen was the same, and with the very same smell he remembered.

"I hope we're not causing you too much trouble," Luís's mother said.

"No, no, *no*! I'm so happy you're here." Eduardo's mother motioned them to the kitchen table and a plate of cookies sitting there. *"Por favor—"*

"Thank you."

Luís found it strange that his mother didn't answer Spanish with Spanish, as she'd been doing with his grandmother. He preferred the way she acted in Las Manos to the way she acted here, in Los Angeles.

He glanced at the window over the sink. His parents' Christmas cactus looked as pathetic as the other one, even in its English pot.

"The neighborhood's changed," he heard his mother say.

"Sí," Eduardo's mother said, going back to her bowl of dough. "It's the war. So many people have moved in— from México! And so many old families have moved out— across the *río*, to the north, to Hollywood, Beverly Hills, Santa Monica. Since Sleepy Lagoon, even more people are talking about moving."

"Sleepy Lagoon?"

"You never heard about Sleepy Lagoon?" Eduardo's mother was shocked.

"No. We didn't have a newspaper in Las Manos, or a radio."

"How did you get *las noticias*?"

"The news? Sometimes we went to Mr. Sandoval's store and listened to him read the newspaper from Las Vegas or Santa Fe."

"*¡Dios mío!* How could you live without news of the war? With your *esposo* fighting and all?"

"What's Sleepy Lagoon?" Luís asked.

"A couple weeks ago, some Mexican kid got killed there in a gang fight, and now everybody thinks every Mexican man is a pachuco with a zoot suit in his closet!"

"Is it safe to live here?" Luís's mother asked.

"*Claro que sí.* The more we Mexicans stick together, the safer we are."

"Where's Eduardo?" Luís asked.

"*No sé,*" Eduardo's mother said, looking down at the dough. "Maybe he's in the garage, working on his bike."

As Luís stood, his mother lifted her hand. "Just a minute, Luís." She turned to Eduardo's mother. "Where should we put our things?"

Eduardo's mother laughed at her own forgetfulness. "You will be with me—*el señor* will sleep on the couch. And Luís will be in Eduardo's *cuarto*, in Fernando's old bed." At the mention of Fernando, she made a sign of the cross, leaving a flour smudge on her forehead.

"Before you go looking for Eduardo, would you take our things to where they belong?"

Paint was peeling off the garage and Eduardo wasn't inside. Neither was his bike. Luís looked at the spot where Eduardo had buried the coffee can filled with money. Was it still there?

Where could Eduardo be? Luís wandered toward the

house where he used to live. The neighborhood had changed all right. There were more Mexican kids and loose dogs playing than he remembered. And the music coming from the open windows of passing cars was often mariachis and *corridos*. How could things have changed so much in such a short time?

His old house looked the same, which seemed odd. How could it be the same with someone else living inside?

He wandered around the neighborhood awhile, taking his time, before starting back to Eduardo's house. Unlike the air of Las Manos, the air here felt heavy and sticky—full of car farts. It clung to him, slowing his sweat as it slid from his armpits and down his ribs. When he glanced up, the sky looked tired, old, caught behind fences made of telephone poles with electric lines strung between.

He turned a corner and, suddenly, the sound of piano music stopped him in his tracks. He found himself standing in front of Stan's house, and—could it be?—the music he heard was the same piece Stan had been practicing nearly nine months ago. Luís smiled. Stan had the mistakes down even better than before.

The music stopped and out the front door flew someone who could have been Stan, if he hadn't been so tall and thin, and if his hair hadn't been so short.

CHAPTER NINETEEN

———◆———

"Hey, Luís! That you?" The voice sounded like Stan's, but lower. And the boy was smiling—Stan's smile on an older boy's face.

"Yeah," Luís said. "That you, Stan?"

"Yeah." Stan came down the porch steps. "I thought you were in New Mexico!"

"I was," Luís said. "But we came back."

"Oh." Stan's smile wavered, and he looked confused.

Luís shrugged, making a show of looking around at the houses. "Things've changed," he said. Was Stan shaving already?

"Yeah."

"You and your family gonna move too? Across the river?"

"Naw," Stan said. "Poppa doesn't wanna live too far from the store, and the store's too big to pick up and move. Says as long as Mexicans wear clothes, we'll stay in business, right on Brooklyn Avenue." His smile returned.

"Whatcha been up to—'cept piano?"

"Nothin' much." He traced a circle with the tip of his shoe on the sidewalk. "I work on airplanes some."

"Airplanes?"

"Models. Wanna see?"

Luís shrugged. "Sure."

He followed Stan around to the side of the house. The cellar doors were flopped open. "I'll get the light," Stan said, disappearing down the groaning stairs.

Luís peered into the darkness. The flash of light was like an explosion without the sound. Luís blinked several times before he could see well enough to enter.

Stan was sitting on a stool next to the furnace, in front of a bench that was hammered together from scraps of wood. Four model airplanes hung from joists in the ceiling. On the bench were pieces of a half-finished model.

"You *made* those?" Luís asked, nodding to the hanging airplanes. They looked real enough to fly out the cellar door.

Stan nodded.

"What's *that* one?" Luís pointed to a plane with wings that looked as if they'd fallen off, cracked in the middle, and been stuck back on with glue that was slowly letting go.

Stan looked up and smiled. "A Stuka. A German dive-bomber." He looked back down. "Your dad fighting in Europe?"

Luís nodded.

"Hope he doesn't run into one of those."

"Why're its wings like that?"

"They're cranked wings—reverse gull wings. They're supposed to look like that. Not like this one." Stan pointed to the one on the bench. "This one's American. A Mustang."

Luís stepped closer, moving so his shadow didn't blot it out. Unlike the Stuka, the Mustang was beautiful. He looked at the ones hanging over his head. "Can they fly?"

Stan nodded. "Yeah. They're powered by rubber bands. But with the war, rubber's gettin' hard to find." He pointed to the plane next to the Stuka. "That's a Mosquito. From England. 'Stead of using a rubber band, I cut a piece of elastic from one of my mother's old girdles." He giggled and Luís smiled. "It's made of balsa wood, just like the real ones. The rest of these are made of heavy paper and cardboard. Since Pearl Harbor, balsa's hard to get. Wanna hold it?"

Luís nodded. Stan stood on the stool and took the airplane off its string. It was surprisingly light and had its own balance, like a boat floating in water. Holding it, he realized that the whole time he'd been in New Mexico, he hadn't seen or heard a single plane in the sky.

They both looked up when they heard footsteps tromp across the floor above their heads.

"Ma-a-an!" Stan groaned. "She's home early, and I'm supposed to be practicing the piano!"

Luís handed the plane to Stan just as they heard the kitchen screen door slap shut.

"Stan? Stan!"

"Coming!" he called.

Luís went up first to let Stan turn off the light.

"What are you doing—" The moment Stan's mother saw Luís, the words stopped.

"Hello, Mrs. Oppenheimer," Luís said.

"Hello, Luís," she said, recovering. "How good to see you!"

"Sorry 'bout the piano, Mom," Stan began. "But—"

His mother shook her head and waved to silence him. "I brought some bagels home from the delicatessen, and they're still warm. Come."

In the kitchen, Luís and Stan watched as Stan's mother sliced a bagel in two and slathered both pieces with cream cheese. "This is great!" Luís said, taking a bite of his half. The smear of cream cheese on his teeth made it easy to smile. "I haven't had one of these since I left!"

"They don't have bagels in New Mexico?" Stan asked.

Luís shook his head and looked from Stan to his mother and back to Stan. What could he get away with? "But they got the best butter in the world."

"Yeah?"

"Yeah. They just run the cows around a field of clover, get their bags really jiggling, so when they milk 'em butter squirts out."

Stan's mother smiled at him and winked. But Stan's eyes grew big as a blob of spilled milk.

With a bagel in his stomach and Stan's voice still echoing in his ears, Luís was almost beginning to feel OK.

150

Walking back to Eduardo's house, he marveled at the palm trees he passed. Their trunks curved upward as gracefully as he remembered. And the twitching skirts of dried leaves below the top still reminded him of girls walking.

Back in the kitchen, both mothers were sitting at the table, still talking. His lungs swelled with the yeasty smell of baking.

Eduardo's mother looked up. "Eduardo's in his *cuarto.*"

He walked down the hall. The door was closed. Opening it, he found himself looking at the startled faces of Eduardo and another boy, both of them sitting on Fernando's bed, Luís's suitcase between them, open.

As Eduardo pulled his hand from the suitcase, the other kid asked, "Don't you ever knock?" Eduardo snickered.

Luís stared. Were they joking around or picking a fight? "Whatcha doin'?" he asked, trying to sound calm.

"Just checkin' to make sure you don't have no *piojos* in your clothes," the other kid said. And then he looked down at Luís's feet. "Nice *pinche* shoes, man. Take 'em off a drunk hobo?"

"Hey, knock it off, Fidel," Eduardo said halfheartedly.

"With pleasure," said Fidel, standing, punching a fist into the palm of his other hand as he swaggered toward Luís.

Luís stuck out his hand. "I'm Luís. What're you doing here?"

The boy's shoulders hunched in surprise and then relaxed. "Nothin'." Hesitating, he put out his hand.

Luís grabbed the hand. Instead of shaking it, he pulled Fidel past him, squeezing hard, walking to his suitcase. "What's goin' on?" he asked, closing it and glaring at Eduardo. "Forgot we're friends?"

"You tell me what's goin' on," Eduardo answered, glaring back. "What the hell you doin' over at Stan's, anyway?"

"You two were spyin' on me?"

Eduardo shrugged. "It's a free country."

"Yeah," Luís said. "It's a free country all right, and that means it don't cost nothin' to be nice to somebody y'haven't seen for a while."

"Ah, blow it out your *pinche*—"

"Look," Luís interrupted. "What you got against Stan, anyway?"

"In case you forgot," Eduardo said, "he's a Jew."

"Yeah," said Fidel from behind. "A Jew *boy!*"

"What d'you know about Jews, anyway?"

"Plenty."

"That so?" Luís said. "Let me feel the top of your head—see if you got those little goat horns."

Eduardo's face grew red. "I ain't no Jew!"

"Then why d'you bury your money in the garage, anyway? Isn't that what Jews do?"

"You callin' me a *Jew*?"

"Something wrong with bein' a Jew?" Luís shot back.

The sound of approaching footsteps caused both of them to look toward the door. It opened just enough for Eduardo's mother's face to poke through.

"*¿Almuerzo?*" She smiled.

Luís hesitated. It had taken him a long time to get used to the people in Las Manos calling breakfast *almuerzo*. "Lunch? Sure."

Her head disappeared.

Eduardo glowered at Luís.

"I think I hear my *ruca* callin'," said Fidel, smiling in a way that reminded Luís of a dog. "See you later, *carnales.*" And then, to Luís's surprise, he hopped onto Fernando's old bed and out the open window. There was a thud and what sounded like cursing. Luís couldn't make out the words.

CHAPTER TWENTY

—◆—

That night, Luís wanted to keep the window over his bed closed. It was too easy for him to imagine Fidel climbing back in, landing on him. But the room got so stuffy and hot that, even with clean sheets and a clean pillowcase, Fernando's old bed stank so much Luís imagined he was lying in a flower garden that every dog in the neighborhood liked to water.

After he opened the window, he was pestered by the sounds of cars. The constant rumbling made him long for the quiet of thick adobe walls and for the sound of air being combed to softness through the needles of piñon and juniper trees.

Frustrated, he sat up and looked out the window, at the sky with its shadowy, dim quarter moon. It reminded him of the afternoon he and Stan and Eduardo had pitched a tent in Stan's backyard to make a fort. The heavy canvas made it dark enough to see pinpricks of sunlight coming through small holes in the cloth. The stars he saw now looked just as fake, and the air coming in through the window smelled almost as mildewy.

His eye caught light skidding over the grime that coated the garage's only window.

Who could be in the garage? The light disappeared. Luís watched a few minutes and, when the light didn't return, he lay down again, thinking it must have been light from a neighbor's window before the shade was drawn.

Luís closed his eyes and tried to sleep. It was difficult. Whenever the car noises died down for a moment, Luís heard Eduardo snoring and mumbling in his sleep. Luís tried to think of something soothing and soon felt sun on his face. Cars began sounding farther away, as if they were racing toward Pasadena, until Luís didn't hear them at all.

The sun was like warm water pooling on his closed eyelids. Las Manos! Where was he—the schoolyard, the *huerta*, the *milpa*, the plaza? He saw himself standing but buried up to his head. He was in the middle of the field between the church and the school.

He tried moving but his arms were pinned to his sides. His chin bumped the ground every time he cried out for help.

He looked around. The field was empty. An ant marched past his face. A coyote cried in the distance. More ants came, swarming, searching for treasure. One crawled up his neck, into his hair. Another crawled around his jaw, onto his face. He shook his head but several more ants crawled aboard.

From nearby a rooster crowed, and a dozen chickens came from nowhere, pecking at the ants around him. Coming closer, they looked at him sideways, anger and greediness in their beady eyes.

Blood drained from his face. The chickens pecked closer and closer. He strained to wiggle his fingers, to loosen the dirt so that he might be able to wriggle his arms free. The dirt pressed tighter. An ant ran into his mouth, and Luís spit it out.

Once more the rooster crowed, closer this time.

"No!"

His shout unnerved the chickens, but only for a moment. They returned to pecking at ants, more frantic than before, drawing closer and closer.

And then, with a tremendous cackle, the rooster jumped onto Luís's head from behind. Talons dug into his scalp as the bird steadied himself. The rooster crowed again and drove his beak into the skin right above Luís's forehead.

Luís screamed as blood crawled through his hair like an ant. The blood trickled down his forehead and slid like grease across his eyebrow, aimed for the outside corner of his eye. From there it dripped big, fat, red tears onto the ground.

The chickens went crazy at the sight of his blood. They rushed toward him, their flapping wings driving dirt into his eyes. He shook his head, trying to topple the rooster, and bellowed. When he threw his face forward, they pecked at his ears and pulled at his hair. The rooster flapped as it danced on his head.

The chickens paused and, in a panic, hopped off Luís and began running in circles, clucking. Sounding strangely timid, the rooster crowed. Luís lifted his head and saw several sleek, low shapes loping at him from different directions.

Before Luís could scream, the rooster shrieked and flew from his head, only to land in front of a coyote. The coyote snapped, catching a wing. Another coyote, growling, jumped from the side, chomping a leg. A third coyote rushed in from the other side, grabbing the other wing. Still the rooster struggled, even as the coyotes pulled him in different directions. Blood spurted from the rooster's shoulder just before a wing snapped off, sounding like cloth tearing. Next, with a popping sound, a leg came off.

Still the bird struggled. Blood flew, splattering onto Luís's face, followed by feathers that stuck to the blood.

From behind came a human voice. "Hey!"

Luís tried turning his head. What was Eduardo doing in Las Manos?

The voice came again, closer. "Hey! Wake up!"

Luís grunted, struggling to free himself from the dirt. His eyes flew open and he found himself looking into Eduardo's angry face. Eduardo was puffing, as if he'd been running, and his eyes almost sizzled. "What'd ya do with it!"

Sweat crawled down Luís's scalp. He shook his head

and shuddered, relieved that he could move his fingers. He took a shaky breath. "Do with what?"

"You know damn, *pinche* well what!"

Luís felt his head, afraid the chickens in his dream had done damage. "I don't know what you're talking about."

"My money," Eduardo growled. "It's gone!"

"What money?" Eduardo's buried money? "*That* money?"

"You're damn, *pinche* right!"

"How should I know?"

"You're the only one who knows about it! Don't make me improve your ugly face! Tell me what you did with it!"

"I'm the only one who knows?" He glared at Eduardo. "What about your friend Fidel?"

"I don't tell him nothing! If I told 'im where the garbage was, he'd steal it! Where is it?" Eduardo took a step closer, his hands balled into fists.

"I don't got it, so cut it out!" Luís threw off the covers and swung his feet over the edge of the bed.

"Where is it?" Eduardo repeated.

"You deaf or something?" Luís stood. "I don't got it, so lay off!" For the first time, Luís realized he was taller than Eduardo, even without shoes on—not much taller, but enough so Eduardo took a step backward.

Eduardo tucked in his chin but kept his angry eyes

on Luís. "You don't stay outta my way, *sapo*," he muttered, "you'll be sorry you ever came back here."

"Don't worry," Luís said, feeling tough, even in his underwear. "Who'd wanna get in your stinkin' way?"

Luís didn't bother going around to the Oppenheimers' kitchen when he saw the cellar doors were flopped open.

He peered beyond the dangling lightbulb. "Stan?"

"Luís? Come help me hold something together."

The air smelled of glue and paint. As he approached the bench, Luís saw the Mustang, looking more like a real plane with paint covering the back of the fuselage.

Stan offered Luís his stool and pointed behind the cockpit of the model. "This front part, it broke off, needs gluing."

"Sure."

"That way I can keep painting. Soon's it's dry, we'll try flying it."

Luís held the piece while Stan squeezed a strand of glue from a tube. It came out thick as spit. Stan smoothed the bead with a toothpick.

"How're things at Eduardo's?" Stan asked, picking up his paintbrush.

Luís was afraid to take his eyes off the piece he was holding. "Not so good."

Stan dipped his brush into a tiny jar of paint. "He's

changed, especially since all the Mexicans started moving in."

"What's wrong with Mexicans?" Luís was sick and tired of everybody badmouthing everybody else.

"Nothing." Stan looked hurt for a moment. "Except Fidel and his gang think they own the neighborhood. That's all. What's he doing to you?"

"Well, this morning he said I stole his money—you know, the money he kept buried in his garage."

Stan went on painting. "He didn't have much. Mostly pennies he stole from his ol' man's pants pockets."

"D'ya know who I think did it?" Stan shook his head. "Fidel!"

"Yeah?" Stan kept painting.

Luís tried to free his finger. It was stuck. "Yeah. Yesterday, when I got back, we had a fight, Eduardo and me. An' Fidel was there when Eduardo was chewin' me out for hanging around with you. And when I asked him why he buried money in his garage if it was a Jew thing, he got pissed." He wiggled his finger, hoping it would break free.

Stan paused in his painting. "What does he have against Jews anyway?"

Embarrassed, Luís looked down at his stuck finger. It all seemed so ridiculous now. "Well, in catechism, Father O'Higgins told us how Jews killed Christ."

"*I* didn't kill Christ."

"Neither did—" Luís stopped himself. "Hey, look, Stan, I glued my finger to the plane."

Stan dropped his brush and grabbed a razor blade. "Happens all the time. Here let me cut it off."

Before Luís could stop him, Stan cut, leaving a shred of skin on the glue. Luís put the finger into his mouth, tasting blood, and farted at the same time.

"Ugh!" Stan gasped, as the round, full sound became a sharp smell. He staggered from Luís and held his nose. "That's some Mexican laughing gas!" He started to laugh.

Luís shook his head and smiled. "I ain't no Mexican. I'm *New* Mexican. And this gas might peel the paint right off—"

"Naw," Stan interrupted. "Wanna play catch while she dries . . . and the stink goes away? Then we can fly her."

CHAPTER TWENTY-ONE

"You've gotten good!" Stan said. Luís caught the ball without even thinking about it.

Luís shrugged. "Not much else to do in Las Manos, 'cept work." He threw the ball back. "Play ball much these days?"

Stan caught the ball and shrugged. "Some. When I can sneak off. Mom's afraid I'll jam a finger, ruin my piano playing." He threw. "But since Fabio and Charlie moved, and Moses and Junho too, Fidel and Eduardo and the other Mexicans won't let me play anyway."

"A Jew thing?" He threw.

Stan nodded, flinching as the ball smacked his palms. "What's it like in your church, anyway?"

"Synagogue?" Stan asked, throwing at the same time.

"Yeah." Luís snagged the ball as it flew over his head.

"Lots of praying and singing. It's peaceful and calm and—and golden." He caught the ball. "It's like—it's like being in this big, beautiful bubble. And then you walk outside and—bam! the bubble bursts." He threw it to Luís. "What's your church like?"

"Mass? About the same. Only you stand up and kneel all the time." He threw. "I like it. A lot."

"Can I come with you to Mass sometime?" Stan threw.

Luís missed and scrambled for the ball. He thought about how he'd been going to Mass all his life—a Jew, at Mass. "Sure." He trotted back with the ball. "Can I go to synagogue sometime with you?" He threw.

"Sure!" Stan smiled, catching. "There's gonna be a famous rabbi this Saturday. All the way from Chicago. Be quite a show." Instead of throwing the ball, he tossed it into the air a couple times. "Gotta practice piano now, 'fore Mom gets home."

Luís groaned.

Stan grinned. "Didn't say how long. Come listen to one song, and if my mother asks you just tell 'er I practiced real good."

Luís glanced at Stan as they walked inside. "Feels good to play with a real ball."

"Yeah?"

"Yeah. Back in Las Manos, the ball we played with was made outta the testicle of a goat."

"No!"

Luís laughed.

Inside, Stan played a piece of music by a guy named Haydn. Luís could hardly believe his ears—Stan didn't make a single mistake that he could tell. And it sounded beautiful.

"Let's go do some flying?" Stan asked, getting up

from the piano stool. "Best place is the Evergreen Cemetery."

Every once in a while Luís smelled something that reminded him of Las Manos. Was it the sun baking parked cars? Or dirt blowing off the occasional dried-up lawn? It was a faint, powdery smell, like sunlight turned to dust, and it made him think of Antonio and miss him. What was he doing now? Harvesting chili? Milking the cow? Sneaking off to a hot spring?

"Any news from your dad?" Stan asked, interrupting these thoughts.

"Not since we got back here," Luís answered.

Stan nodded. "You know Moses joined up?"

"No!" Luís checked Stan's face to see if Stan was getting even for the goat testicle. "He's not old enough!"

"Lied about his age. Said he'd eat bacon and ham every day if he could fight the Nazis. Guess he had some relatives there who lost everything 'cause of Hitler."

They were getting within sight of the cemetery.

"You have relatives there? In Europe?"

"Naw." Stan was cradling the airplane in the crook of an arm and started stroking it, as if it were a cat. "We came from Russia. The ones that didn't get out were killed in a pogrom."

"Jeez! Why does anybody stay a *pinche* Jew, anyway—what with everybody wanting to kill 'em?"

They walked into the cemetery. Stan shrugged.

"Search me." He pointed. "That's the best place. Over there."

They passed through the part of the cemetery where many of the gravestones had photographs of people fixed on porcelain disks. Luís had always found it spooky to stare at pictures of the faces of people who were buried.

They came to the top of a rise and stopped. The cemetery's grass was dried and yellow, making the cemetery itself look like a dead thing.

"You hold it, and I'll crank it up," said Stan.

Little puffs of breeze brought the plane to life in Luís's hands. It twitched as if it were trying to escape. Stan wound the propeller until the rubber band squeaked.

Holding the propeller, Stan said, "OK, now. Lift the nose a little. That's right. Now, into the wind some more. That's right. Now—" Stan ducked and let go. The plane leapt from Luís's hands, wobbling until it gained speed. The propeller sounded like a beater in whipped cream until it suddenly stopped.

"Wow!" Luís watched the plane glide, riding the air like a boat on water. It veered toward the right.

"Let's get it before it crashes!" Stan trotted down the rise, weaving in and out of gravestones. Luís was close behind.

Each flight, though different, was magical. Luís and Stan took turns cranking the propeller and aiming the plane. For the next half hour Luís forgot where he was. The city seemed to have melted away. The only sound he heard was the propeller beating the air. The only thing he saw was the plane's shape against the sky, looking as if it were real.

So when the plane banked left, drifting toward two boys, Luís was surprised to see that he and Stan weren't alone.

"Eduardo!" Luís gasped.

"And Fidel! Better get the plane 'fore they do!"

As the plane approached, Eduardo took two steps sideways and grabbed it out of the air.

"Hey!" Stan shouted. "Get your mitts off my plane!"

Fidel took the plane from Eduardo and hid it behind his back. "What plane?"

"Playing with your Jew friend? Again?" Eduardo hissed.

"Give it back." Stan spoke quietly and held his hand out to Fidel.

"Make you a deal," Eduardo said to Luís. "Give back my money and I see you get the *pinche* plane back in one piece."

"I don't have your money!" Luís turned to Fidel and glared. "What did *you* do with it, *pocho*?"

"*¿Pocho?*" Fidel whipped the plane out from behind his back and poked it at Luís. "You call me a *pocho*?"

"Stop that!" Stan cried, grabbing for it. Fidel pulled it back, cradling it in the crook of one arm.

"I don't like being called no *pocho*," Fidel said, all quiet now. He handed the plane to Eduardo and stepped toward Luís. "Wanna take it back?"

Luís hesitated, not wanting to fight, but not wanting to take anything back either. Fidel went for Luís's knees. Luís stepped out of the way, almost bumping into Eduardo, who pushed him with a free hand, sending him stumbling to the ground.

"Stay outta their fight!" Stan barked. "Two against one ain't fair!"

Eduardo growled, "Shut your trap!" But he took a step backward.

Luís scrambled to his feet and whirled around. Fidel was coming at him, a fist held high. He dodged but not enough, and Fidel's fist landed on his shoulder.

"Hey!" He grabbed Fidel's arm and, grunting and twisting, yanked.

"Yeow!" Fidel shouted. He kicked Luís on a shin.

It was as if his body knew what to do before his head did. Luís grabbed Fidel's other arm, pulled the older boy toward him, and swung a leg behind Fidel's knees, pushing out. Fidel's legs collapsed. He fell backward, his head bouncing on the grass, just missing a gravestone. Luís dropped onto Fidel's chest, pinning his arms with his knees.

Luís was surprised at how easy it was to hold Fidel down, even though Fidel twisted and spit and tried to buck him off. All the work in the *milpas* and *huertas* had made him hard as the clay he'd plowed and tough as the weeds he'd pulled.

"What'd you do with it?" Luís said.

Fidel tried to butt his head against Luís's stomach. When that didn't work, he tried spitting again. He missed and a glob of spittle landed on his own face, sliding down the side of his nose.

"I know you took it! You were listening to Eduardo and me. And then last night, I saw lights in the garage!" He looked down at Fidel's red face, jerking from side to side, and decided to take a chance. "I *saw* you! I saw you leave the garage!"

"Did not!" Fidel screamed, the veins bulging on the sides of his neck. "Nobody saw us!" He bared his teeth and arched his back.

"Us?" Eduardo sounded surprised and hurt.

Fidel grew still as he realized the mistake he'd just made.

"Who was with you?"

This time Fidel looked at Eduardo. "You think *I* took your stinkin' money?"

Eduardo stared.

Fidel turned back to Luís. "Get your smelly butt off me!" Fidel was close to tears, and Luís wanted him to cry.

"What you doin' hanging around with a Jew, anyway, 'stead of your homeboys?" Fidel blurted, looking at Luís. "Neighborhood's changed!"

"Yeah?" Stan stepped toward Fidel and Luís. "It's still *my* neighborhood too."

Fidel turned his head toward Eduardo. "Don't just stand there! Do something!"

Eduardo didn't move.

"*Do* something!"

Still Eduardo didn't move. "Just stay outta my face," he said, quietly, turning and walking away.

"Wait 'til your brother finds out!" Fidel called after him. "Finds out you turned your back on a homeboy—that you're a Jew lover!"

"Shut your mouth," Luís said, leaning his full weight on Fidel's arms. Fidel winced and shut his mouth. "I think Fernando's gonna be upset when he finds out that you stole from his brother. Don't do nothin' funny," Luís said, and he pushed himself off Fidel, off to the side in case Fidel tried kicking him in the nuts.

Fidel scrambled to his feet and glared at Stan. "You'll never see me in your poppa's store again!" he said.

"That's OK by me," Stan said. "There are plenty of people around Brooklyn Avenue who don't need to buy things with stolen money. Your poppa's one of 'em."

Fidel looked as if he'd been slugged. "Leave my poppa out of it!" He turned and stumbled down the hill, his shoulders hunched, rubbing his arms where Luís had pinned him.

Eduardo was quiet throughout dinner and all evening. When Luís decided it was time for bed, he was surprised to see Eduardo already under the covers, his face turned toward the wall.

"Feeling OK?" Luís asked from Fernando's old bed.

Eduardo just lay there.

"Wanna help fly a plane tomorrow?"

Eduardo stirred. Slowly he turned to face Luís, who was shocked to see that Eduardo had been crying.

"Look, you—you *pinche* jerk," Eduardo said. "So what about Fidel? I shoulda known. But don't get any *pinche* ideas. You wanna be my friend, you gotta dump Stan. It's Stan or me. Can't be both."

Luís began untying his shoes. One of the bows had turned into a knot. Still working the knot, he looked up at Eduardo. "Look, *sapo,* you're not gonna tell me who I can be friends with. Maybe we'll never be friends again, you and me, but you're not gonna blame *me* for that. You don't wanna be my friend, fine. But I'm Stan's friend." The knot dissolved in his hands. "And I wouldn't mind being your friend too."

Eduardo grunted and turned his back to Luís.

CHAPTER TWENTY-TWO

"Think He's watching?" Eduardo gasped as he ran behind Luís.

"He sees everything, don't He?" Luís wished he weren't wearing a tie. "Even on Saturday?"

"I still think we shoulda asked Father O'Higgins if this is a sin."

"How could it be a sin to go to a church?"

"It's not a church, *carnal*. It's a synagogue. *Sin*-agogue—get it?"

Luís groaned. "How d'you know God's not a Jew too? Christ was." Luís ran faster, testing to see if Eduardo could keep up. He did.

"'Cause he's already Catholic, that why—and if he was a Jew too, it'd mess up his whole *pinche* weekend going to synagogue on Saturday and Mass on Sunday!"

Luís shook his head as he ran. Sometimes he wondered if Eduardo had ridden a merry-go-round too much as a kid.

They turned onto Breen Street. Stan was pacing in front of the synagogue. When he spotted them, he waved, a big smile on his face, his head looking funny with his beanie smashing down his hair.

"Where you guys been? It's almost ready to start."

Luís shrugged. "We had to stop at our church, ask God to forgive us."

Stan shook his head at such a stupid joke and handed them each a yarmulke. "Here," he said. "Gotta put one on. Don't worry. We'll be in back. Just do what I do."

Luís hesitated. What would he find inside? What if it was disappointing? What if it was great? Would he tell Stan his secret? Start going to both synagogue and Mass? That would sure mess up his whole weekend! Luís wished Uncle Solomón was around to talk to. Or his father. Especially his father. Maybe later today he'd write a letter to his father. He'd been wanting to for the longest time, and his mother had been bugging him to do it for months.

He glanced up at the big stained-glass window above the door. It was in shadow and didn't look blue or yellow or any other color. Star of David. Six points. Two triangles. What was the big deal? It might as well be a Star of Luís. And why not? It was pretty. It was an easy star to make. And he liked it.

"Come on!" Stan pulled open the door.

Making the sign of the cross, Luís took a step toward the mouth of the synagogue. Why am I holding my breath? he asked himself. And then he knew. He'd felt like this each time in the split second before he hit the snow-water of the *acequia* in Las Manos—excited, tense, braced for the shock, but totally alive.

Letting the air out in a *whoosh,* Luís followed Stan inside, Eduardo's puffing close behind.

SPANISH WORDS AND PHRASES

———◆———

The Spanish spoken in Los Angeles in the 1940s was influenced by Spanish brought northward from Mexico, which in turn was influenced by Mexican Indian languages. The Spanish spoken in the villages of northern New Mexico at that time (and now) was made up of the old Castilian Spanish of the 1500s, Mexican Indian words (mainly Nahuatl), Indian words from the New Mexico pueblos, Mexican Spanish, and English that New Mexicans borrowed and adapted for everyday use. A good source for understanding this rich and fascinating Spanish dialect is *A Dictionary of New Mexico and Southern Colorado Spanish*, Rubén Cobos (Museum of New Mexico Press). New Mexico idioms are noted with an (NM).

abuela [ah-bway'-la] grandmother
abuelo [ah-bway'-lo] grandfather
acequia [ah-say'-key-ah] an irrigation ditch
al gallo [all guy'-yo] to the rooster
almuerzo [all-mwear'-so] lunch; breakfast (NM)

atole [ah-toll'-ay] a gruel or mush made by mixing water and ground corn

baile [buy'-lay] dance

basura [baa-sue'-rah] garbage

bien [beeyen] good

bienvenido [beeyen-ven-ee'-doe] welcome

bizcochito [beese-coe-chee'-toe] a type of sugar cookie flavored with anise found in northern New Mexico

boracho [bo-rah'-choe] drunk

bribón [bree-bone'] rascal or rogue

bueno [bway'-noh] good

buenos días [bway'-nohs dee'-ahs] good day, hello

cabrón [ka-brone'] son of a goat (NM)

calabazas [cah-lah-bah-sahs] pumpkins

camposanto [cam-po-san'-toe] cemetery

carnal [car-nal'] brother or sister, as in friend (NM), from Spanish for flesh and blood

carne seca [car'-nay say'-ca] dried strips of meat, plain, pickled, or cured in salt

chingón [cheen-gohn'] wow (NM)

Cinco Rosas [seen'-coe roe'-sas] Five Roses hair tonic

claro que sí [cla'-roh kay see] of course, clearly

¿cómo está, Padre? [koe'-moe eh-stah' pa'-dray] how are you, Father?

¿cómo se dice? [koe'-moe say dee'-say] how do you say . . . ?

como yo otra vez [koe'-moe yo oh'-tra vase] like me, again

comprende [comb-pren'-day] understand

compuertas [comb-pwair'-tas] gates to control the flow of water from an irrigation ditch

corrida del gallo [coe-ree'-dah dell guy'-yo] a rooster pull (NM), coming from the antiquated Spanish word corrida for flowing, as in water or blood

corridos [coe-ree'-dose] romantic and popular Spanish ballad

coyotes [ko-yo'-tays] Spanish pronunciation for coyotes, prairie wolves found from Alaska to Costa Rica, from Los Angeles to Maine

cuarto [kwar'-toe] room, bedroom (slang)

cucarachas [coo-ca-rah'-chas] cockroaches

cute [coo'-tay] jacket or overcoat (NM), from English coat

de nada [day nah'-dah] it's nothing

de veras [day ver'-as] truthfully

Dios mío [dee'-ohs mee'-oh] my God (exclamation)

dólares [doe'-lah-race] dollars

el baile [el buy'-lay] the dance

el día de Santiago [el dee'-ah day san-tee-ah'-go] the feast day of Saint James the Apostle, July 25

el señor [el say-nyor'] the mister

el viejo [el vee-ay'-ho] the old man (often affectionate)

ese [ess'-ay] buddy (slang)

esposo [ess-po´-so] husband

estás aquí [es-tahs´ ah-key´] you are here

esto es mi hijo [es´-toe es me ee´-ho] this is my son

fiesta [fee-es´-tah] party, celebration

flojo [flow´-ho] lazy or timid person (slang)

fon [phone] fun (NM), from English fun

fracasada [fra-kah-sah´-dah] dented, as in a car fender (NM)

gabacho [gah-bah´-cho] gringo, Anglo-American

gallo [guy´-yo] rooster

gracias [gra´-see-ahs] thanks

gracias a Dios [gra´-see-ahs ah dee´-ohs] thanks to God

habla español [ah´-blah eh-spa-nyoll´] speak Spanish

hablo español, un poquito [ah´-blow eh-spa-nyoll´ oon poe-key´-toe] I speak Spanish, a little

hola, hijos [oh´-la, ee´-hos] hello, boys (or children)

horno [or´-no] large beehive-shaped outdoor oven

huerta [wear´-tah] vegetable garden; chili field (NM)

hueso [way´-so] bone; children's game using cow bones (NM)

huevos [way´-vos] eggs, testicles (slang)

incréible [een-cray-ee´-blay] incredible

judío [who-dee´-oh] Jew

la Ciudad de los Angeles [la seeyou-dahd´ day los ahn-hay-lace] the city of angels, Los Angeles

La Llorona [la yo-row′-nah] the wailing woman of Latino folklore

la muchachada [la moo-chah-cha′-dah] a gang of boys or girls

la raza [la rah′saw] the people, as in Latinos

la vieja [la vee-ay′-ha] the old woman (often affectionate)

las noticias [las no-tee′-see-yas] the news

leña [lay′-nyah] wood, chopped for burning

listo [lee′-stow] ready

lonche [lone′-chay] lunch (NM), from English lunch

madre [mah′-dray] mother

mamá [mah-sah′] momma

mamacita [mah-mah-see′-tah] mother (affectionate)

mañana [mah-nyah′-nah] tomorrow

mantequilla [mahn-tay-key′-yah] butter

mariachis [mah-ree-ah′-cheese] a type of music originating in Mexico, lively and loud and emotional

masa [mah′-sah] dough, usually made with corn flour, for tamales

matador de Cristo [mah-tah-door′ day cree′-stow] Christ-killer, often used as an insult to Jews

medicina [may-dee-see′-nah] medicine

México [may′-he-koh] Mexico, Spanish pronunciation

mi nieto [me kneeay′-toe] my grandson

m'jito [may-he′-toe] my son (affectionate)

milpa [meal'-pah] cornfield

mira [me'-rah] look

mole [moh'-lay] a Mexican sauce made from chili and chocolate, usually served with chicken or pork

mula [moo'-lah] homemade corn liquor

Nuevo México [nway'-voe may'-he-koh] New Mexico

otro gallo [oh'-tro guy'-yo] another rooster

pachuco [pah-choo'-co] a member of a gang of young men and boys who wear zoot suits; a punk or a tough guy (slang)

Padre [pah'-dray] Father, as in priest; father

papi [pa-pea'] father (affectionate)

pinche [peen'-chay] crummy, damned, worthless

piojos [peeoh'-hose] lice, nits

pocho [poh'-cho] Mexican American (insult)

por favor [pore fa-vore'] please

pues [pways] well, then

qué lindo [kay lean'-doh] how pretty

río [ree'-oh] river

ruca [roo'-cah] girlfriend (slang)

sapo [sah'-poh] toad, chubby person (NM)

señora [say-nyo'-rah] ma'am, missus

sí [see] yes

son judíos [sone who-deeohs'] they are Jews

tamales [tah-maul'-ayes] cornmeal dough stuffed with ground, seasoned meat (or raisins or fruit) and steamed

tienen hambre [teean'-en ahm'-bray] are you hungry? or: they are hungry

tío [tee'-oh] uncle

velís [vay-lease] heads up! (NM)

ven acá [ven ah-kaw] come

About the Author

MARC TALBERT has written ten novels for young people, most recently *Heart of the Jaguar* (Simon & Schuster). This is his first book for Clarion. Of *Star of Luís,* he says, "Often what families reveal about themselves is less interesting than what they keep secret. Luís and I share a heritage we didn't know about until after we thought we knew who we were and where our families came from." Mr. Talbert lives in an adobe house in Tesuque, New Mexico, with his wife and two daughters.